About the Author

My name is Charlie. I have been writing for longer than I remember, and it has been a dream to one day see my work in print. Life has thrown a lot at me over the years, and being able to hide within a fantasy world, whether one I created or worlds created by other authors, gave me the strength to continue. I hope that my book is able to give someone the break from reality that they need one day, too!

A Family Born

Charlie Hardy

A Family Born

Olympia Publishers
London

www.olympiapublishers.com
OLYMPIA PAPERBACK EDITION

A CIP catalogue record for this title is
available from the British Library.

ISBN: 978-1-80074-565-0

This is a work of fiction.
Names, characters, places and incidents originate from the writer's
imagination. Any resemblance to actual persons, living or dead, is
purely coincidental.

First Published in 2022

Olympia Publishers
Tallis House
2 Tallis Street
London
EC4Y 0AB

Printed in Great Britain

Dedication

I dedicate this book to my husband and family and my close
friends in Carp Corp.

Acknowledgements

Thank-you to my husband and family, who always supported me, and to Carp Corp who pushed me to carry on.

Chapter 1

In a far-off land, from miles apart, two people met. One man, Silent; an anarchist with a thirst for violence. One person, Paradox; a builder looking for a protector.

The day they found each other should be remembered as a day that history was made.

Together, they began exploring a world full of dangers and mysteries. Over time, the two became closer, forming bonds deeper than friendship. Needing each other, they agreed to enter into the platonic union of marriage and became the platonic couple that you will be able to hear about here. For this is the story of a created family.

Some months into their platonic marriage, tragedy struck; they were sucked from their world, being spat out into a world where nothing looked familiar. It left them with no food, no tools, no armour, and perhaps most sadly, no home. They had lived life travelling their previous world, where they had secret stacks of resources in different areas. But here they had no back up, no safety net and nothing to rely on but each other. Instinctively knowing that there was no way back to where they had previously been, Paradox decided that it was time to put down some roots and make the most of the situation. After spending several hours, searching the area where they had landed, the two of them found an area with fresh green grass, with animals grazing that they could farm, a forest area for a supply of wood, and a quarry beneath them for stone and possibly other resources.

Agreeing that it was a good area, the two made a crude shelter for protection from any dangers that might be in the world around them, and began to work out what building materials they would need in order to not only survive, but thrive in the area.

Being travellers, naturally, they both had excellent survival skills. While Silent was the main defender, often the protagonist in many confrontations, he was skilled enough with a sword and other weapons to win. He was also a dab hand at farming. Paradox on the other hand was a master craftsman. They could create anything, given the right resources, and their building skills were unrivalled. They also had a natural charm about them, meaning they often found that trading with villages they passed in their travels went much smoother if they were the one talking... You know, and not waving a sword around...

To start with, they gathered some loose wood, and created a table that was sturdy enough to craft useful objects on. The first thing Paradox created was a wooden pickaxe. Quickly heading to some nearby exposed stone, they painstakingly dug into the stone, collecting a dozen useable pieces. Returning to the crafting table, they started to fashion a stone axe for chopping down trees. Handing the finished product to Silent, he swiftly made his way into the forest.

Knowing that they would need to wait for Silent to return with more wood to be able to make any more tools, Paradox started to use some of the remaining stone to create a forge, knowing that they would need it for smelting and cooking further down the line. As Silent was going to be a while, and relying on stone to chop down the trees, Paradox returned to the exposed stone from earlier and started to dig further. The additional material would make things hopefully run smoother in the future. Digging down, and creating rough steps as they went, aware that any additional resource that might be available here would be slightly deeper, Paradox started to realise that the area was getting darker as they hollowed out the cave. Suddenly, they struck something that wasn't rock. Collecting the piece that chipped off, they walked with it to the entrance so that they could see it in the daylight.

Delighted, they could see that it was a piece of coal. Knowing that it would be a valuable resource, they returned to the dark, feeling along the walls for the change of texture, and mining the vein of coal. Once they could no longer feel any more coal, they returned to the light and the crafting table.

They had managed to gather two large stacks of what looked to be cobblestone, and about fifty pieces of coal. By this point, it was getting dark, and knowing the dangers of the area, they started to move towards the makeshift hut they had. Hearing movement in the distance, they turned, hoping that Silent was returning. Shocked and scared, they could see a humanoid figure stumbling towards them... that was not the way Silent moved.

After taking the axe from Paradox, Silent quickly moved into the forest. Knowing that they wanted to make this place somewhere they could stay forever, Silent wanted to leave resources to grow back rather than decimate the area entirely. Deciding to chop down every fourth tree, he quickly set to work. Feeling the axe bite into the wood of the first tree, Silent quickly settled into a rhythm, chopping the tree into sizable chunks and destroying any leafy branches. Occasionally, he would strike lucky and an apple would fall from a branch. Making sure that he stored them carefully, he continued, gathering the sticks that sometimes dropped. Once a tree had been destroyed, if there was a sapling that had been part of the tree, he would make sure to plant it before moving on to the next tree.

After some time, he had almost as much wood as he could carry, a good, few apples, and some sticks. Looking at the sky through the leaves above, he realised that it was starting to get dark, and that he should make his way home to Paradox. Still holding his axe, he started back, heard a rattle, and spun to look behind him. Shock filled him and his heart sunk. Standing in the shade of a tree, facing away from him and holding a bow and arrows, was a skeleton. Not understanding what voodoo had created this, he started to back away, creeping to avoid being seen, unknowing if it would attack. Hearing another rattle behind him, he jumped, accidentally stepping on a loose stick, which gave a deafening crack. The skeleton in front of him turned, and on seeing him, drew back the bow, arrow notched. As it aimed, he risked a glance behind him, seeing the second skeleton also drawing a bow. As he tried to work out the best direction to run in, a sharp pain hit his shoulder. The first skeleton had loosed the arrow. Dropping to one knee at the unexpected pain proved to be the best choice, as the arrow from the second skeleton flew over his head, accidentally striking the first one. This proved to be a blessing in disguise, as the two then started to fight each other, giving Silent enough time to pull himself to his feet and readjust his grip on the axe. He decided that if he ran, they may give chase; and he was not one to run from a fight, no matter the odds. Within seconds, it was over. One skeleton became a pile of bones, a bow, and some arrows, and the other, now injured, turned to Silent. Running towards it, he tried to reach it before it could draw another arrow — but Silent was a little too slow, delayed by his injured shoulder. The arrow left the bow, and Silent blocked it with his injured arm, using his good arm to swing a blow at the already injured skeleton. Two swings of his axe were all it took to kill the creature. Taking a breath, he could see that there were about four salvageable arrows and two bows. One had a damaged string, the other had a crack in the upper limb. Quickly picking up the arrows, he realised that to grab the bow, he was going to have to leave some of the wood; but knowing that it was worth it, he removed the string from the bow with the damaged limb, and restrung this string onto the other bow, leaving him with one bow in fairly good condition.

Walking much faster now, but unwilling to run and put pressure on his bad shoulder — especially if there were more dangers and he may need to use the bow — he headed for home, very conscious of the darkening sky.

Paradox hoped that the figure was friendly, but started to back towards their hut, knowing that they had no defence, and the only offense was a very damaged wooden pickaxe. As they were steadily backing away, the final ray of sunlight peered through a gap in the treeline, lighting the area around the figure, and Paradox saw a shambling attempt at a man, with rotting skin, and angry dead eyes. The zombie, for it could be nothing else, walked through a patch of sunlight, and *caught fire*!

It was still shambling towards them, but slower now. Suddenly, an arrow appeared through the head of the zombie, and it dropped, burning out and leaving nothing but a few bits of rotten, slightly charred flesh. Looking in the direction the arrow came from, they saw a sight that lifted their heart, only for it to fall again. Silent was back, but he seemed to be trying to emulate a porcupine. Two arrows were protruding from his shoulder, meeting him halfway, and checking that he was going to be okay, Paradox took the wood and sticks that he was carrying, put the wood with the stone, and helped Silent into their makeshift house. Using one of the sticks, and one lump of coal, they managed to make four torches which they put in each corner of the hut, brightening the area. After ensuring that the door was as secure as it was going to be, they helped Silent to sit down, and pulled the arrows carefully from his shoulder and arm, distracting each other by talking through what they had managed to accomplish with their day. Using some of their shirt to bind the wounds, Paradox then took some of the apples for them both to eat and restore their strength, giving Silent slightly more to help him heal quicker. Luckily, both being far from human, with enough food, they both would heal in a matter of minutes. Seeing Silent relax as the pain faded, they settled in for a long night, without a bed; sleep was not going to happen quickly. They took the time to study the creatures that seemed to have appeared with the darkness.

The skeletons seemed willing to fight anything and had an unlimited supply of arrows; once or twice, Silent could swear he saw one of them riding on the back of one of the giant spiders. There had been a couple of those spiders in the woods, and they had left him alone, so either they were only active at night, or they only caused issues as the mount of a skeleton. There appeared to be three distinctive types of zombies; one smaller, which was much faster, one large and slow which they had seen earlier wearing torn turquoise t-shirts and ragged blue trousers, and one very similar but dressed in clothes that seemed to indicate some kind of trade. Do the zombies turn people from local villages? If they do, can they be restored?

There also seemed to be some type of creature that hissed as it walked along. For the first few hours of the night, nothing could really be told about them. Suddenly, one of them walked into the path of an arrow that was aimed at another skeleton. Changing direction, the creeper headed to the skeleton that had shot at it and... exploded?

"Oooh explodey boi's!"

Laughing at Silent's comment, Paradox started to try and figure out uses for the things they could gather from these creatures, considering what weapons and armour they would need. Ideally, they would want to get a hold of some iron, but would need some better stone tools to mine that far, if there was any in the quarry by them. Minds racing with thoughts and plans, they suddenly saw something that they didn't expect, something that could be amazingly beneficial if they could find it.

"Honey!"

"Hmm? Yes dear?" was the response from Silent.

Laughing at him thinking they were using pet names for him, Paradox explained that they had seen some bees, and that meant there would be honey somewhere.

Focusing back to outside, they didn't notice Silent move from his watch hole until he sat down next to them.

"Dox Darling, it is going to be okay!"

"That is going to be a thing now, isn't it? I give you a pet name one time and now I have an alliteration of a nickname?"

Grinning, Silent nodded.

"Let's try to get some sleep. Tomorrow is going to be busy."

After one of the worst night's sleeps they had ever had, the platonic partners rose with the sun. Looking outside, they saw the skeletons and zombies burning in the sun. The few spiders seemed content to just sit in the sun, and there seemed to only be one of the green creepers. Knowing that Dox was better and faster with a bow, Silent handed it to them, both agreeing that they should try to kill the creeper rather than have it threaten the precious resources that they have gathered. With Silent holding his axe, prepared to back up Dox if needed, they opened the door.

As it was facing away from them, Dox took aim, and hit the creeper. It turned, spotting them, and started to head in their direction. Quickly aiming with the second arrow, they once again shot and hit. Sadly, it kept coming. Knowing that this was their last arrow, and it was getting closer, Silent tightened his grip on the axe. As the final arrow flew and hit, finally the creeper fell, dissolving into some type of powder. Letting out a breath, they moved further away from the door, keeping an eye on the spiders, which seemed happy to ignore them. Gathering some of the powder, they realised that it was some type of gun powder, which would explain the explosions. Stowing it with the rest of their things, Dox quickly set to work on the crafting table, making a couple of large chests to store their limited supplies in. They then took the first chunk of wood, realising that they should be able to make about four planks from each chunk, and then four good sticks from each plank. Leaving a couple of stacks of the wood whole, they quickly broke the rest of the wood into planks and some of the planks into sticks.

Leaving the planks for a moment, Dox then took some of the coal, sticks and stone, making two stacks of torches, followed by three stone pickaxes, a stone hoe and a stone shovel. Having known each other for so long, words were no longer needed. Silent took one of the stacks of torches, the three pickaxes, and headed to the start of the mining tunnel which Dox had started the previous day.

Knowing that he would be gone for a while, or until he found something, Dox started to combine the sticks and planks to make fencing, deciding that blocking off the area that they wanted to build on should be a priority for the day. Anything to keep out the awful creatures that seemed to appear in this place. Once created, they took the fencing with them, encircling the entire area, and mentally planning for an area to have a farm; somewhere for the house, and somewhere for some livestock. After making sure that the area was protected, they decided to place torches around the area, both within and outside of the fence line, theorising that if these creatures didn't like the sun, they might avoid lit up areas too… at least a little bit.

Knowing that they were at least somewhat protected, they took the shovel and started to level the area. A little while into it, they cleared out a bit of brush, and as they destroyed it, noticed that there were some seeds left over. After examining them, they realised that they were some type of wheat seed. Excitedly moving back over to the storage area to grab the hoe, they quickly had the ground prepared, and the seed planted — and that was when they realised what was missing from the fenced area… water. There was a small lake a very short distance away, but they had no way to collect the water.

Hoping that Silent would manage to find some iron, they dug out a few areas ready for when they had a bucket, or something, and continued levelling the area, gathering all of the seeds as they went.

Chapter 2

Meanwhile, Silent was digging steadily, placing torches as he went. So far, he had gathered several stacks of coal, cobblestone, diorite and granite. Glad that he thought to bring one of the chests, he made sure to return to the entrance where he had left the chest to deposit them occasionally. Suddenly, Silent noticed something glinting through the block he was about to break. Iron! Finally. Carefully mining the ore, he could see that the vein continued. Swiftly mining it out, he could see that there was probably enough for nine ingots if they were careful. Moving towards the daylight, Silent decided that the quicker they could get it smelting, the better. As he returned to the surface, he could see that Dox was levelling the ground at the other side of the area, and that they had fenced the entire area. Smiling to himself, he put the ore into the furnace that had been created yesterday and used some of the coal he had mined to light it. While waiting for it to smelt, he made a couple of extra stone pickaxes before he walked over to Dox to give them an update.

Together, they made their way back to the furnace, with Dox suggesting that they use the first two ingots to make a bucket so that they could collect water, another two to make a sword, a sharper, longer lasting pickaxe could be the next three, and if there was enough, to use some of the planks and an ingot for each to make two shields. Agreeing with his platonic partner, he checked the furnace to see that there were indeed nine ingots and that they had finished smelting. Pulling out the ingots, he handed them over to Dox, who made the first shield with planks and one ingot, a sword out of two ingots and one of the sticks, and a pickaxe out of the next three and a stick for the handle. While working, Silent suggested that he use the stone pickaxes, for standard stone and coal, but the iron one if they come across any more ore, or anything new. Agreeing, Dox passed the items to Silent, who smiled and left to return to mining.

Using the remaining ore for another shield and a bucket, Dox realised that in their haste to create a fence, they had not made a gate. Quickly putting one together, and ignoring the fact that it was slightly lopsided, they grabbed Silent's very worn axe and headed to the side closest to the water. Chopping one section down with the axe was successful, but was too much for the axe, and it shattered on the final hit. Attaching and fastening the gate, they moved through the gateway and made sure it was closed and headed to the water. Scooping up a bucket full of water, they headed back to the fence, entering through the gate and heading to the start of the farm. Tipping the water into the pre-prepared hole, they watched with satisfaction as the ground darkened as the water seeped in. Knowing that they would have quite a few trips to make, they continued, carefully securing the gate on the last trip. They were satisfied with the distribution of water for the farm, and the small artificial pond that prevented too many excess trips.

Planting the rest of the seeds that they had found, they were happy to see that things were growing speedily. Continuing with levelling the area, they started to mentally plan what they wanted to do with the house. The abundance of stone that they would have from mining made it the obvious choice of building material, with wood for decoration, flooring, and the roof.

Completing the levelling of the area, they started to mark out the floor plan for the ground floor of the house. Wanting a large kitchen area, a dining room… wait, what if we make it like a tavern? If we were randomly dropped here, there are likely to be other travellers. We could run a bit of a way station, a safe area for people to come. If they are like us, they could come here to start up, and having nothing on them, they could owe us a future favour that we could cash in when we wanted. It would be a fighting free zone; no weapons allowed, and armour stays at the door or in their rooms. Lost in thoughts of future plans, they slowly mapped out the large floor plan, slowly raised the height of the walls and built a crude staircase to allow them to scale up and down the walls without injuring themselves. At the mid-way point of the walls, they planned to have the floor of the second storey. Scaling down now that the walls were at a good height, they returned to the crafting table, and noticed that there was now a second furnace that seemed to have smelted gold in it, now cold, and a large stack of iron in the other one. There was some type of red powder in one of the chests and something blue in another one.

Grabbing the iron, they started to make some armour, knowing that defending themselves was a priority. Trying to make things as even as possible, they used the first sixteen ingots to make each of them a breast plate, the next fourteen to make two iron leggings, then ten to make a pair of helmets, and finally eight to make two pairs of boots. There were still sixteen ingots left over which, for now, they put safely in a chest, along with Silent's set of armour.

Grabbing some of the wooden planks and moving to the crafting table, Dox set about turning them into slabs, finding that if they used three of the planks, they could make six slabs. Once a couple of stacks had been made, they returned to the shell of a house and added the flooring to the ground floor, before climbing halfway up the stairs and starting to lay the flooring for the second floor. They quickly found that the easiest and safest way was to lay one slab, crouch, shuffle to the edge to lay the next one along, and repeat. Needing to be careful not to fall, the second-floor flooring took twice as long, and it looked like it was starting to get dark.

Climbing back down the stairs, Dox heard the sound of a sheep in the distance. Suddenly having an idea, they hurried to the crafting table and used two of the remaining iron to fashion a set of shears. Checking that there was still some daylight left, they left the enclosure through the gate, and started to look for the sheep. Halfway between the enclosed area and the forest stood four sheep, grazing. Hurrying over to them, they quickly sheered them, collecting the wool. As they finished the last sheep, full dark hit. Hearing a rattle from the trees, Dox headed quickly back to the enclosure. Reaching the gate just ahead of a small zombie, they were able to get the gate shut and step back. Breathing a sigh of relief, they headed back to the crafting table. After taking two steps away, they stumbled forwards in pain, an arrow lodged firmly in their leg. A fence was only as good as the height of it, and they were still in sight of the skeleton that was now standing by the water on the other side of the fence. Limping towards the crafting table, they moved as quick as possible to get out of reach of the arrows before another was shot. Checking, they could see that they had gathered nine pieces of wool, and for the beds they wanted to make, they would only need six. Storing the extra three, they could use six wool and six planks to create two beds. Moving into the entrance of their house, Dox decided to wait for Silent to return to help take out the arrow to make sure that they didn't do any more damage.

Back down in the mine, Silent has managed to find an abundance of iron, plenty of coal and more cobblestone than they could possibly need. With a final swing of his third stone pickaxe, Silent could see that he had broken through to some type of cavern; however, with that final swing, the pickaxe had also shattered. Deciding to make a run to the surface, he made sure he had everything he could carry, wondering about the strange dark blue substance and the red powder that he had found down there. Happy with the fact that he had a stack of sixty-four iron blocks, and about fifteen blocks that seemed to be gold, Silent hit the surface, and filled the furnace with the iron, adding more coal and lighting it. He then decided to create a second furnace and set the gold to smelting as well.

Spending the extra time to create several more torches and five additional stone pickaxes, he looked over to where Dox had placed an outline of an *extremely* large house... there was only the two of them, did they need that much space? As he turned to head back, he could see that there was a wheat crop growing on what must have been the start of a much larger plot for farming. Noticing that some of the crop was ready to harvest, he changed direction and harvested the ripe crop, replanting the seeds that had dropped into the already prepared earth. For each plant collected, there seemed to have been about three seeds dropped, allowing him to plant several additional sections, and take the nine pieces of ripe crop back to drop off in the chests.

Returning back to his tunnel, he headed to the bottom of his staircase and peered into the hole he had made. Nearly dropping his torch in shock, he could see that he had mined right into... a mine.

Unable to believe his luck, he quickly shored up a path from his ledge onto the wooden platform that seemed to be set up for miners to walk on when working. Going by the amount of spider's webs and the lack of people, the mineshaft looked to be abandoned. It could be because it was empty of ore now, but going by the amount he had found tunnelling down to this point, he didn't think so. It probably meant that there was something dangerous that caused people to leave. Going by the monsters on the surface, he could believe that. Deciding to be careful, he started to explore the area, placing torches on the left-hand side of his route so that if he had the torches on the right, he would know he was heading back to his path up. Making sure to mine any and all resource blocks as he passed, he collected quite a stack of gold and iron ore alongside so much coal, the strange red stone and a little of the blue. A few minutes into exploring he heard the groan of a zombie. Pulling out his sword, he proceeded with a little more care, rounding a final corner to come face to face with two zombies. Quickly jumping into battle, he took a couple of hits, but was able to kill them. Taking a breath, he took out an apple, and quickly ate it to speed his healing. Continuing on down the corridor, he came across a chest. Opening it, he couldn't quite believe his luck. There was some kind of glowing book called Depth Strider III, five diamonds and three potatoes. Grabbing his loot, Silent decided not to push his luck, and turned around to start to head back. Knowing that it must have been nearly dark by now, Silent wanted to make sure that he and Dox were together. Despite knowing that they were now in a fenced off area, there was no harm in being too careful. Reaching the gap that led back up to the stairs, Silent sealed up the gap, not wanting any of the monsters to be able to follow him out of the mine and up to the house.

Making it to the top of the stairs, he walked across to the furnace, set the gold and iron to smelting, put the rest of the materials in the chest, and he made his way to the house. That Dox had managed to put up the walls, floor and ceiling in such a short amount of time was impressive. Entering through the open doorway, he saw Dox standing next to two beds… with an arrow in their leg.

Hurrying over to them and making sure that they were okay, he helped them sit on the edge of the bed pulled out the arrow, bandaged the wound, and made sure they ate one of the final few apples. Catching each other up on their respective days, they both agreed that, after having no decent sleep the night before, they should get some sleep, and worry about tomorrow when it came. Safe in their new home for the first time, on a comfortable bed, both quickly fell asleep.

Chapter 3

The next morning, the two sat to discuss what their plans for the day were. Dox had planned to make the roof for the house, and to start to add some details. If they had time, they also wanted to try to herd some of the animals into the enclosure so that they could have the start of a farm.

Silent did not want to return to the darkness of the mine for a second day in a row, and decided that he would explore some of the surrounding areas. Needing to have more information about what surrounded them, finding out what other potential resources they could find was imperative. If they were lucky, there might be a village nearby that they could visit to find out some information about where they were.

"Oh?" said Silent, looking up from where he was checking his sword.

"Yes, if you find a village just... don't talk to anyone? Better yet, don't even go in, just remember where it is and come and get me?"

"Hey! I am not that bad! I can easily go into a village and get information!"

"Silent, torturing villagers for Intel is not the same thing. We both know that you have a shady background, and that you won't talk about it, but violence isn't always the answer!"

Silent opened his mouth to respond.

"And don't you dare say it is the question, because I will resort to violence if I need to."

Silent closed his mouth with a pout.

"Fine, Dox Darling! I promise not to go into any villages without you."

"Thank you, Honey!"

Laughing softly at each other, Dox lead Silent back down to the crafting table and handed him the armour that they made yesterday. While Silent pulled the armour on, Dox started to take the iron and gold out of the forge, and noticed that the iron hadn't quite finished smelting before the coal had run out. Adding some more and relighting it, they turned back to Silent to see them pulling the helmet onto their head, and then strapping the shield to their arm. Making a snap decision and quickly crafting him an axe as a backup, they turned to Silent to hand it to him.

"Oh, Silent, what did you want me to do with the diamonds? We probably have enough to make a sword and a pickaxe, or a helmet, or boots? I don't think it would work for a shield, as it is mostly wood and wouldn't combine well, and there won't be enough for anything else I don't think, except maybe an axe?"

"Probably a sword and pickaxe. Or two swords, and that way we both have the same offensive weapons?"

"Oh no, I am happy with my bow, thank you very much! You are the one who likes a close quarters fight. I would rather stay safe in my house or fight from a distance!"

Chuckling at them, knowing that it is true, Silent agrees to the sword and pickaxe.

Quickly grabbing two of the diamonds and one stick, Dox crafts a sword, swapping it for the iron sword Silent was carrying, and attaching the iron sword to their own belt before moving on to create the pickaxe.

Giving the sword a few practice swirls, Silent admired the way the light reflected off the blue hue of the sword.

"Ooh, Shiny **stabby** stick!"

"Yes, dear… now be safe and don't get lost. While I would like to see you back home tonight, I think we both know that it won't happen. But try to head back and check in before too long. If it's been over a week, I will assume you have perished and shall be forced to move on with life without you!"

Laughing, Silent sheathed the sword and headed towards the gate. Shoving slightly at the lopsided slant to it, he managed to open it, slipped through, and securely fastened it again. Calling out goodbye over his shoulder, he set off at a bouncy run, following the fence line towards the forest and north. On the off chance that he returned in the dark, he placed torches down along his path to ensure that he could make it back.

For a while, he passed nothing of interest, until he heard the sound of someone coming his way. A man, leading two llamas, headed straight for him. Loosening his sword just in case, he said hello to the man. The man turns out to be a wandering trader, who traded in a specific type of shell. Upon finding out that Silent had nothing to trade, he made a rude remark about peasants and shoulder barged passed him. Rage at the comment had Silent spinning around after the man, pulling out the sword and cutting him down where he stood. Not expecting llamas to be protective, he was shocked when they both started to attack him. Reacting instinctively, he fought back, killing them both. One positive note on this is that, although the man actually had nothing on him, Silent was able to take skin from the llamas to dry into leather and meat. He also noticed that there were two leads that had clearly been used for the llamas.

Taking the time to set the skin out to dry, hanging from a wooden frame he could attach to his back while he could carry on exploring, he continued.

Shortly after, he passed beyond the oak tree line to come to some sort of flower field. Thinking that Dox would appreciate some of the flowers, he decided that on the way home he would collect some for them. If he dug them out at the roots, they would be able to replant them. If they were going to create the house as a way station or tavern, then maybe they could make some flowerpots for the rooms to go on the windowsills.

Enjoying the smell of the flowers, Silent almost missed the egg before he stepped on it, catching himself as he felt something different under his foot. Looking around, he spotted a few more. Gathering them up and storing them, he continued. On the far side of the flower fields, he saw what looked to be a man-made path. Deciding to follow it, he suddenly spotted the roof of a house in the distance… many houses. Excited, he picked up speed, hurrying to the first of the houses before suddenly jerking to a stop. His promise to Dox still fresh on his mind, he reluctantly turned to the left and skirted around the edge of the village, noting that it had taken him less than half a day of travel to arrive. He knew that he still had a couple of hours left until night, and so he set off, still heading north. He soon entered another wooded area; this time the trees seemed to be birch. Listening to the sounds of the woods, he suddenly heard the sound of a sheep in the distance. Having an idea, he bounded off in the direction of the sound, pulling out his sword as he ran. Locating the sheep, he saw that there were four of them. Picking the two closest to him, he quickly dispatched them, watching the other two run away. He then sheared away the wool and took the meat. Using some fallen wood, he created a rudimentary crafting table before going to the nearest birch tree, taking out his axe, and making short work to get a chunk of wood.

Taking the wood to the crafting table, he stripped it into four planks, and used three of them and the wool to create a portable bed. Storing the portable bed, he left the crafting table where it was and continued on, still placing torches as he went.

As he got to the end of the birch woods, he could see that it appeared to be some kind of swamp that he was entering. As it looked like it was getting dark, and knowing that the monsters seemed to appear at night, he created a rudimentary shelter, placed down his bed, and settled in for the night.

Waking up in the morning was a bit of an experience. He could hear the rattle of skeletons, the crackle of the flames as they burned, and a strange *Vroomph* noise. Gathering his bed and knocking down the shelter, he looked around in time to see four skeletons drop and disintegrate, flames petering out, leaving behind bones and arrows. Hearing the sound again, he saw a large black shape holding a block of dirt. Carefully watching the creature as it seemed to ignore him, he jumped in shock as the creature made the noise again and **disappeared!** Looking around, he saw it on the far side of where his shelter was. He decided that if the creature was going to ignore him, he would ignore it. Walking over to where the closest skeleton had collapsed, he gathered both the bones and the arrows, deciding that Dox might be able to find a use for them.

Checking for his path of torches behind him and seeing that he had gone through a stack of them at this point, he faced north once again and set off. Judging by the way the swamp looked, he was going to have to wade through a lot of this, with brief island stops on route. Taking his first step into the cold water, he winced as he felt it seep into his armoured boots, sodden up to his knees. Accepting fate, he started moving forwards, deciding that it would be warmer if he kept moving. Reaching the first island, he once again placed a torch, looking around. There are some types of trees on the island, with thick vines falling down to the floor. Walking to the nearest tree, he tested the vine, establishing that it would take his weight, and pulled himself up, scaling up to the top of the tree. Carefully placing his feet to ensure that the top of the tree would hold him, he used the vantage point to look forward to see if there was anything visible from there that would be worth heading towards. Sadly, being unable to see anything beyond more swamp, he returned to ground level and continued on. Once again returning to wade through the swampy cold water, he continued north. Seeing the water start to clear, he realised that he was nearing the edge of the swamp. Glad to be able to leave the water for a while and hopefully dry off, he saw that beyond the last swampy tree, the land opened up into a vast plane. Wading through the water had slowed him down considerably, and by now the sun was starting to set again. With the fading light, Silent swiftly moved from the edge of the swamp and onto the open plane, seeing a large hole open ahead of him, It looked like something had exploded.

"Ahh, an explodey boi!"

Scurrying down into the hole, he laid out his bed, ate his last apple to regain strength and laid down to sleep. Feeling extremely exposed, sleep was slow to claim him. He heard the occasional hiss of a spider that passed, or the groan of a zombie. Finally, after an eternity of laying still, hoping that he didn't make a sound that would alert the monsters to his presence, he drifted off into a dream filled sleep.

He is flying. The air is cold and burns his lungs as he soars through the clouds. Wanting a drink, he swoops down, landing gracefully. As he kneels down to drink, something solid slams into the back of his head. Knocking him forwards, his head swims, collapsing onto his arms, nearly face planting the water. Before he can clear his head, he hears snorting, almost pig-like, and hands grab his arms, legs, and head, immobilising him. He feels the cold touch of steel on his shoulders, followed by the most excruciating pain of his life, and then nothing, as he finally succumbs to the pain and passes out.

Gasping for air, Silent bolted upright from his bed, heart pounding and tears streaming down his face. Swinging himself into a kneeling position, he stripped off his breastplate, hands instinctively crossing to the opposite shoulder, and ran his fingers over the raised scar tissue there. Eyes burning, he tried to blink away the memories; the pain of awakening with his wings gone. The emotional pain was more than any physical pain could come close to. Taking a fortifying breath, he lifted his hands from his shoulders and wiped his eyes.

It had been months since he last had that dream. He had thought that he was finally at peace from it.

He had made a mistake that day. He hadn't looked at his surrounding area, and there had been a strange portal just within the tree line. A portal that led to somewhere of fire and death. Pig-like humans had come through to his world, creatures with an obsession with gold. Apparently, the golden flecks that had highlighted the green of his wings had been too much for the creatures to resist as they had seen him gliding down to the water's edge, and they had attacked. He had been a peaceful being until that point. However, after feeling so helpless, after being unable to save himself and then losing his most important ability — a part of him — he turned to violence.

He became learned in the art of war, of fighting, with any weapon or with no weapon, against multiple opponents or someone stronger than him. His life became nothing but daily training and nightly terrors. He became a mercenary for hire, not caring about the funding as much as the target. He would never harm someone innocent, always doing his own research into any job. And then he found Dox. His Paradox.

He had finished a job, but got caught by a potion as he left. It was some kind of weakening potion, and while he knew his body could pull through it, he had nowhere safe to hide. As he stumbled around the edge of a house, he bumped into someone. Looking up at the person who went with the hand that had caught him, he saw a soft, kind pair of purple eyes.

"Are you ok?"

The voice was quiet but firm. Trying to speak didn't seem to be working for Silent; a garbled attempt at language fell out of his mouth, and for the second time in his life, he passed out.

Coming too, he felt warm and comfortable. Blinking, he sat up. Looking around, he was in a small room furnished as a kitchen, bedroom, and lounge. Everything was cramped in together; one large door that looked like it would lead outside, and one much smaller narrow door that he assumed would lead to the bathroom. At that point, the main door opened, and the person walked in.

"Oh, you are awake. How are you feeling?"

"Ummmm," was the most intelligent response he could come up with.

Seeming to realise that Silence was still trying to process things, the person started to ramble about unimportant things; apologising for basically kidnapping him, randomly talking about the amount of rain that had been happening, telling him that he could stay for as long as he needed, asking if he was hungry, and a host of other things that filled the silence around him. He blinked at the number of words being spoken, but realised that despite how much the other was speaking, nothing of importance was said.

"You really are a paradox, aren't you? You realise that you are not supposed to take the sketchy looking stranger back to your house to help them, right? You also don't then apologise for helping them!"

They cut themselves off at the sound of his voice, and grinned over at him. "A paradox. I like that. I was looking for a new name, and I think that will do quite nicely."

Returning to pottering around the kitchen, they soon brought over some soup and a glass of water for Silent.

Blinking back to the present, Silent realised it was that day that he met Dox that his nightmares had stopped. He hadn't noticed at the time, but from that initial meeting, he hadn't gone a day without meeting them at least once, and within a couple of months they had been inseparable. A family. There had never been anything romantic between them, but they bickered like an old married couple. He wasn't sure who made the first joke that they might as well be married, but after so long, with neither having any inclination to find a romantic attachment, they accepted that they were just a platonically married couple. Two people closer than friends.

Standing, he gathered his things, crawled out of his hole and headed for home.

He needed Dox.

Chapter 4

They watched until Silent was out of sight, hoping that he wouldn't be gone too long. While they may have joked about the week, since meeting, they hadn't spent more than forty-eight hours apart.

The day they met had been the best day that Paradox had had in a long time. Once, they had lived in a small family community. They were immigrants from a different world, and one day Paradox had awoken to an empty house, and a note saying that the family had returned home, and that as the youngest, they felt that Paradox would adjust better to life here, and that they didn't want to take that away from them.

They had left in the middle of the night, knowing that if given the option, Paradox would have followed to stay with family. Alone and scared, they wandered the streets of the small village that they were in, and tried to come up with a plan. Thinking through, they knew that logically, they needed to sell the house that they were in. They had no source of income alone, and it was much too big for them. It hadn't taken long for someone to buy it, and they had then moved into a tiny cottage, more of a shack. They had felt numb since reading the letter. In shock. The day they moved, they had to cram everything from their last life into such a small space

When they were finally alone, the front door shut to their new house, the numbness lifted, and the reality finally kicked in. Sinking to their knees, the feeling of catastrophic loneliness forced its way down their throat and seemed to rip their heart out of their stomach. A gut-wrenching sob tore out of their throat, and once one released, it was like the flood gates opened. Sobs wracked their body, finally able to process the grief.

After a few hours, the sobs died down, exhaustion sank in, and emotionally and physically wrung out, they fell asleep there on the floor of their new house... no longer a home, because they were alone.

The next day they awoke, stood up, and stretched, back stiff from the bedroom floor. Taking two steps over to the kitchen counter, they grabbed a glass from the box on the side where it had been left still packed from the move the day before. Turning on the cold-water tap, they filled the glass, raised it to their lips and drained it. Not realizing how parched they were, they quickly refilled and again drained the glass. Filling it for the third time, they took a long mouthful, and placed the glass on the side. Looking around the tiny room, they couldn't help the small sigh of regret, already missing the open spaces of home, only cluttered by people and love.

Knowing that they couldn't spend time moping around, they started to dig out the clothes that they would need to work that day. Rather than having a stable job, they worked for a small business doing odd jobs and repairs.

And so became the new normal; wake up, drink water and eat, go to work and complete any requested tasks, go home, eat dinner, and sleep, repeat — not knowing who they were, or what they were doing with their life. Their name, their family name causes nothing but pain to hear it. A constant reminder that they were alone.

Until that one day. Walking home late from work, there was a small commotion, like someone was stumbling. Turning the

37

corner, they walked into a man, a man who stumbled backwards.
Reaching out a hand, they grabbed his arm and the man looked
up, meeting their eyes with his green ones. Those eyes looked like
they had seen too much to be looking out of a young face.

"Are you ok?"

A stupid question to ask; he gave a garbled response before
collapsing and passing out.

Left with two choices, they could leave the man and get help,
or they could take him back to theirs, just round the corner...
okay, so they were never going to do the first one.

Gripping his arm a little tighter, they hoisted his slightly
larger frame over their shoulder and started to make their way
slowly towards their door. It was slow going, with the man's feet
dragging on the floor behind them. Making it to the door, they
shuffled their grip to be able to open the door, almost falling
through it as it finally swung open. Managing to catch the two of
them before they could hit the floor, they steadied themselves on
the door frame before taking the two steps to the bed and
unceremoniously dumping the man on it. Taking a quick breather,
they pulled the man up a little further on the bed, positioning his
arms and legs into a more natural position. Looking at his face,
they could see a slightly orange substance on his skin. Grabbing
a washcloth from the clean pile of clothes and wetting it in the
sink, they rinsed off his face, clearing the substance away. Almost
immediately his colour looked a little better. Pulling the covers
over him, they decided that they would probably sleep best on the
small chair in the corner. Grabbing a pillow and a spare blanket,
they curled up to nap. As expected, they did not sleep well, and
awoke early, deciding that a short walk would help to clear their
head. After walking, enjoying the cool early morning mist, they
returned to their house, opened the front door and glanced

towards the bed. They were shocked to see that the man had awoken.

Blinking back the memories, Dox turned to focus on the task at hand. Building a house, a home for them. Turning to the stack of wood, mentally planning out what the next best thing would be, they decided that they needed to get the stairs up and running, hating the current stone ledges that they had put in as a temporary measure. Taking some of the logs to the crafting table, they quickly stripped them into planks before turning the planks into stairs. The two small alcoves they had made at the front would be used for guest storage, and to make the stairs. They decided that the left alcove, if you were looking from the doorway, would be for the stairs; a wooden winding staircase set into the alcove, which would stretch up into the ceiling, allowing access to a loft. Finishing the final step, they replaced the excess logs into the chest, noticing that at the bottom of the chest was three potatoes. Excited, they grabbed them and ran over to the small farm that was growing. Planting the potatoes on the far side of the patch, they ensured that the ground was saturated and near enough to the water for a speedy growth. Looking over at the wheat, they could see that it was all ready to be harvested, and that the patch looked larger than before. They knew that Silent had probably harvested some at some point, and knowing him, he wouldn't have seen doing something nice or helpful as something worth mentioning. Shaking their head fondly, they gathered the harvest. Replanting all the seeds that fell, they were able to double the size of the farm. Pleased with their work, they headed back over to the crafting table and chests and placed the wheat into a chest, deciding that they could probably make some bread with it later. Making sure that all of the steps were gathered up, they headed to the house and quickly set to work on the staircase. Watching it come together as the staircase turned each corner to become a spiral was satisfying, and once they reached the first floor, they used some of the left-over slabs from the previous day to shore up the top section of the stairs, ensuring that everything was structurally sound. Deciding to leave a flat platform for the first floor, so that there were no steps in the middle of the landing, they continued the stairs after a platform, the next step being one facing the back wall. Finally reaching the height that they would want the ceiling of that floor to be, they began using the last of the slabs they had, keeping crouched to make sure they didn't tumble from the edge. Despite knowing that while in the armour the fall wouldn't damage them too much, it still wasn't something that they would like to experience. Managing to stretch the slabs to cover just over a third of the area, they let out a sigh, realizing that they would need to go and make more slabs, and then try to work out what they wanted to do about the roof. The roof would need to go on next; they had been lucky with the weather so far and hadn't had any rain, but the last thing they wanted was to have water damage to the house. Thinking about it, it should have really been the second thing to do after the walls, but the challenge of scaling the walls from the ground just added to the risk.

Climbing down the stairs and heading back to the crafting area, they decided then that they would make both slabs and some more stair-like sections, theorising that the right-angle that they sit at would look very aesthetically pleasing. After so long spent creating things, both items and buildings, they had long since come to trust their initial judgement. Loosing themselves in the monotonous creation of slabs and steps, they thought back to the second time they had met Silent.

Silent had stayed to recuperate for another day after he first awoke, and after the initial introduction, he had lived up to his name, looking around in silence. And this man. Honestly the most infuriating being to walk the lands, without even opening his mouth. He held an air of arrogance, as if he was simply better than everyone else. This attitude created an instant dislike in them, and for one moment, they thought that if instead of grabbing his arm, they had let him stumble back, dropping to the floor and leaving him there, they would have a peaceful night, without this man cluttering up their already limited space. It was like his eyes were judging everything in sight. In a desire to end the oppressive and awkward silence, they had spoken about a great many things, nothing of importance, but just as a way to lift the suffocating silence filling the small space. Watching him leave had been such a relief, thankful that they would not have to deal with his presence again.

The next morning, they headed to work, looking forward to getting back to some normality. Pulling on a leather apron, they started to tinker with some of the items that they had been trying to create. They wanted to make some kind of device to track the hours as they passed, allowing someone who wasn't able to look outside to tell what the time was, and if it was daylight still or not. They had made the workings of it, but needed some kind of reactive ingredient that would make it function. Hearing someone enter, they briefly looked up before returning to their work, knowing that the owner of the shop would deal with any customer, having only provided them with this work to do. Vaguely hearing muffled voices in the background, they continued with what they were doing. A few minutes later, the owner, a gruff burly man with a bush brown beard and a bald head, simply known as The Architect, walked into their work room.

"We have a customer that wants something designed and created to help him. He is a traveller, and wants some kind of device to allow him to carry many heavy things with him. He has the natural strength to carry things, just not a way to store them."

Putting down the device, and thinking, they considered the building and creating magic that was in this world. So different from their own, but just as useful in some cases.

"I could probably design some sort of storage container, with specific sections in it, allowing multiple of the same object to take up the same space? Like if you stack coins on top of each other, and look down at them from above, you can only see the top one. The space would only take up one object, but the weight would consist of all of them."

Considering the possibility, they started to ramble, going into the technical and magical things that would need to be created, allowing for multiple things to exist within the same space.

"Okay then!" The Architect cut them off quickly. "I am going to leave you to discuss the particulars with the client. I will send him back to you." And he left, not giving them a chance to stop him, a level of panic about having to speak to an unknown person starting to rise within them. The panic was swiftly replaced with irritation as Silent walked into their work room.

In obviously feigned shock, he took a dramatic step closer.

"Paradox?! What are you doing here? Do you work here?"

Reminding themself that he was a paying customer, they took a slow calming breath, and put what hopefully looked like a smile on.

"Hello again. It is nice to see you are doing better still. I wasn't expecting to see you again so soon."

Or ever.

"So, you want to be able to carry your full limit of weight without actually having to hold all of the items, is that right?"

As Silent agreed, they allowed themselves to relax a little, starting to discuss the technical thought process that they had started. Beginning to map out a plan, they started to sketch out some details, stopping to pause as Silent asked what sort of limit there would be on how many items could stack within the same space. Shocked but pleased that for once, someone was not only following their tangent without zoning out, but had actually asked a valid question, they continued, advising that the weight, density, and a few other factors would decide how much could be carried. Organic matter like an egg for example, would take up more room than a stack of wood, and while you would be able to carry a stack of buckets, if they had water in them, they would have to be separate.

Several hours passed in this way, bouncing details back and forth, agreeing a plan, with Silent advising that he would come back in the afternoon the next day to see how things were going. Saying goodbye, they watched as he left their workroom to head through the shop to the door. Hearing the door shut, they felt a slight pang of loss. For the first time in months, they noticed that the icy, lonely wasteland that their heart had become thawed slightly.

Their interactions had continued in that way for weeks; Silent discovering something that they wanted made and coming to Paradox, the two of them talking through the details of what and how, and Silent checking in daily. About three months in, Silent had come to the shop, his mood clearly low, and told Dox that they were having to head out on the road and that they didn't know when they would be back. Joking to try and lighten the mood, he mentioned that he didn't know what he would do without someone to create some of his random ideas, or to fix the things he broke when he was training. Joking back, they suggested that they would need a portable Paradox, laughing outwardly, but already feeling the loss of their companionship.

They froze at the suddenly predatory look in Silent's eyes as he stalked around the crafting table to look down at them, using the extra 3.5 inches of height to his advantage.

"Yes."

"Ummmm, yes what, Silent? You can't just say 'yes' and expect me to know what you are saying yes to."

"Yes, I need a portable Paradox! And you... you are portable. Come with me!"

"Whaa... what do you mean come with you? Just drop life here, gather my things, and travel this world, fixing and creating things along the way to make some money?" Laughing at the idea, they tried to look away from the excitement shining within those neon green eyes they had come to know so well. A cold hand grabbed at their heart as they saw some of that bright excitement dim.

Silent took a small step back, eyes dropping from Paradox's face, the bravado front cracking slightly, before his insecure mask of arrogance settled around him.

"Well, it was an idea and an offer only. Obviously, there is no expectation on you."

Mind racing, Paradox considered the offer, actually looking at it as a genuine possibility. They had a house that they slept in, but there was no attachment there, they had their job, but most of what they did was work for Silent, and if he leaves, The Architect might downsize, leaving them without a job. They didn't have any personal attachment here. And if Silent left, he might never come back, And Paradox didn't think they could lose someone else close to them.

While they had been considering the options, they hadn't noticed Silent back away from them, and softly leave the work room. They didn't notice until they heard the main door open. Head snapping up, Silent's name tumbled from their lips, calling out for him to wait. Rounding the corner to the main room, they saw him paused, head high, eyes cold, with one hand on the door handle, door half open.

"When do we leave?"

Finishing the last log of wood, Paradox returned to the present, a slight smile on their face at the memory of their best decision: to follow Silent where he wandered.

Chapter 5

Gathering together the slabs and steps, they headed towards the house. On route, they noticed that the wheat and potatoes seemed to be ready for harvest. Making a small detour, they quickly harvested and replanted, once again doubling the size of the wheat crop. For the potato crop, they decided to replant everything they had gathered, allowing them to triple the size of it. Moving towards the house, they were grateful for the speed that things seemed to grow here. In all their travels with Silent, they had found places where a single crop would take weeks or months to grow to ripeness, and if this place had been like that, they would not have been able to survive, let alone thrive, as Dox was planning for them to do here. Back in the house, they moved their way up the stairs, crouching down and laying the slabs to make the ceiling. Realizing as they stood up that it was getting dark, they made their way back down the stairs, and heading to their bed they settled in for the night. They fell into a dreamless sleep quickly, which considering the active day they had, was not surprising.

A violent explosion shocked them from their sleep, bolting upright and sprinting for the hole in the house wall, cursing themselves for not already making a door. The sun was just starting to peek above the horizon, giving them just enough light to see that one of the exploding creeping things had exploded the far corner of their fence. Seeing this, they realised that a skeleton was making its way towards the gap. Realizing that their bow was sitting uselessly in one of the chests by the crafting table, they grabbed their shield and strapped it to their arm before pulling out Silent's old sword. Hearing the rattle drawing closer, they focused back just in time to catch an arrow on the shield. Sprinting forwards a few steps while the skeleton reloaded, they closed the distance between them, pausing to take the next arrow on the shield. On the next reload, they managed to fully close the distance, take one final arrow on the shield and swing the sword at the skeleton. Already damaged from the explosion, one strong hit was enough to collapse it, leaving behind a couple of functioning arrows, some bone and a very damaged bow. Gathering everything together, they moved to the chests, collecting their bow, and making sure to keep the arrows with them. Finding a couple of left-over fence panels and some of the dirt that they had left over from when they were levelling the area, they were able to fill in the hole made by the explosion and repair the fence line. As they attached the last section of fence, the line of sunlight finally reached them, and they listened to the symphony sounds of things on fire as the remaining skeletons and zombies burnt with the light. Deciding to go and see if there were any surviving arrows from the skeletons later, they returned to the crafting table. Fixing their nearly catastrophic oversight, they pulled together two doors from the oak planks, carried them to the house, and firmly attached both, to make a nice double door entrance.

Climbing the stairs, they decided that they should be able to get the roof put together quite quickly. Alternating between the slabs and the steps, they were able to create a slanted but sturdy roof, angling in to meet at a point down the centre. As the last piece was placed, the room was plunged into darkness, and realising that they had not really considered a light source, they placed some torches on the walls, brightening things up a little more. Contemplating creating some type of lantern that they could hang from the ceiling, they realised that they did not have nearly enough iron for that at this point.

Heading downstairs again, they made a point to add a few extra torches. Wanting to leave the downstairs fairly open planned, they marked out an area that would be the kitchen, and using the few oak planks they still had on them, created a bar area, leaving a section open, allowing people to pass through to get behind it. Heading outside, they realised that once again the crops were ready for harvest. Again, being able to double the wheat and triple the potatoes gave Dox hope that before too long, they would easily be able to help others to get on their feet if needed, or to just host travellers. Holding the wheat, they headed along the fence line, thinking about what they would need next. A sudden *moo* from next to them made them jump. Following them along the fence, staring longingly at the wheat, was a cow. Looking between the cow and the wheat, Dox was struck with an idea. Being that these animals were clearly wild, rather than needing to trade with a village, they could round up and breed and farm these. It would be easy enough to gather some cows if the way this one was looking at the wheat was anything to go by.

Making a snap decision, they grabbed the last of the fence panels, quickly created a gate, and created a large pen in the far corner of their enclosure. Checking the area outside, to ensure that there were no monsters lurking, they opened both gates and headed outside. Quickly spotting the cow standing with a second cow just the other side of several sheep, they made their way over to them. Pulling out the wheat, they suddenly had the attention of not only the two cows, but each of the sheep as well.

Holding the wheat away from their body, they slowly started

to make their way to the first gate. Like a herd, the cows and sheep slowly moved with them. Making it through the gate, a sudden pile up halted progress as all of the animals tried to get through at once. After a moment, they had all made it through. Quickly circling around them, they got the first gate shut, making sure nothing else could get in, and none of their new animals could escape. They repeated the process, herding them towards the pen, and waiting for the pile up to clear before slipping out of the gate and closing it. Making sure to feed each of the animals some wheat, they turned back towards the house. It had been a long but successful day, and as the sky darkened, they looked towards the north, sighing at the pang of loneliness.

Silent had been making good time on his route home. Wading through the swamp much quicker having a set direction, and being able to follow the path of his torches, he only paused to collect things that he thought might be of use to Dox. The first time he stopped, he had veered slightly off course, and seen a tall reed-like plant at the edge of the swamp. Carefully breaking it from the bottom, each tall plant easily split into three manageable chunks. Gathering just under a stack and storing it carefully, he headed off again, smiling at the thought of his pack. Specially designed by Dox, he had expected to be laughed at, and told that what he wanted was impossible. He came up with the idea as a last-minute desire to see the Dox that had looked after him. Someone who was kind but didn't want him for anything, who never asked for anything in return. A kind being? A Dox if ever he had seen one. But then they did the impossible and created it for him. And so, he went away again, delighted with what they had created, but without a reason to return. A pattern followed, him trying to come up with more creative and impossible things for them to struggle with, and their talents throwing away his efforts to stump them and creating his every thought. The day he thought he would lose them — when he was called to a job that would require months of travel — ended up being the happiest of his life when they agreed to travel with him.

Continuing on his way through the birch woods, avoiding the village, he reached the next torch, finding himself back within the flower fields. Gathering many of them, he decided that they may be able to make dyes from them, and the only reason he was gathering so many of the purple ones was because he preferred darker colour, and absolutely nothing to do with the colour of their eyes.

After decimating the flower field, although leaving enough behind so that they would be able to re-pollenate and continue growing, he carried on. The urge to get home was growing stronger. He had been running for well over half of the day by this point, and had to pause to eat the last apple he had. After replenishing his strength, he carried on.

As the sky started to darken, he realised that he was not going to make it home before full dark, however he had no intention of sleeping. Knowing that his nightmare was lying in wait for him to close his eyes, it reminded him of why he spent so many years as an insomniac, only falling asleep when his body and mind were on the brink of collapse, and there was no energy for those memories to haunt him. Continuing forwards, knowing that his entire priority right now was to get home, he pushed himself harder, returning to his jumping sprint that would launch him forward, and gaining more speed by lengthening the distance he took per step.

He finally reached the oak forest, just as full dark arrived. Carefully listening out for danger, he used the light of the torches previously placed to make his way, their light ensuring that he could see enough of the ground to avoid stumbling over something. The tell-tale rattle of a skeleton came from his left, followed by the *thwunk* of an arrow as it missed his head and buried itself in a nearby tree. Contemplating stopping to attack the creature, he realised that it would only slow him down, and from what he had seen, they were unable to do much more than walk. Shaking off the thought, he picked up speed again. Passing by a multitude of rattles and groans, he tried to ignore the urge to eradicate the threat. He was a mature person, and he could easily stop the urge to murder… right?

Suddenly he heard the scramble of fast paced feet, and from the right, one of the small zombies catapulted themselves at him. Blocking the attack with his shield, he quickly drew his sword just in time to hit back the second attack. Heart racing, he saw it returning for a third attack. As he prepared, he heard an ominous hissing from behind. Changing tactic, he deflected the attack to send the creature past him, preferring to have both enemies on the same side of him. As he turned, he saw one of the explosive creatures, right next to where the small zombie was turning back to attack again. The creature was puffing up, the hissing intensifying. Changing his grip so that his focus was on his shield, he took two quick steps back. The explosion rocked the area, thankfully killing the small zombie, but also knocking him back several paces, sapping his energy. Pushing himself to his feet, and brushing himself off, he turned to continue home. While his pace was noticeably slower now, he was determined to keep moving, unwilling to accept defeat in a forest so close to home. Slowly, the trees started to thin out, and finally, in the distance was the warm welcoming light of home.

Waking alone again on the third day of Silent's adventure, Dox decided that they would try to get as much of the interior of the house sorted as they could. Knowing what Silent was like when he attempted to cook, they decided not to use wooden walls, but to use some of the large quantity of stone. Heading to the crafting table, they grabbed some wooden planks for the interior walls upstairs, and some stone for the kitchen. Starting to head back to the house, they suddenly paused, walked back, grabbed as much wood and stone as possible, and grabbed the crafting table, extremely glad that they had created their own travel storage before starting their adventures with Silent. Walking back to the house, they placed the crafting table down, and decided that rather than a storage chest, barrel-like cupboards would work much better. Using some of the cobblestone, they quickly put together a wall, separating the kitchen from the main room and leaving a gap for a door. Next, using some of the planks and left-over slabs, they created about thirty barrels, much more than they currently needed, but it allowed them to place them at the top of the walls on three sides of the room.

Taking some more of the stone, they put together some more furnaces, knowing that they would be useful both for cooking food and for any smelting that needed to happen. They placed the furnaces around the crafting table where it was sat on the left-hand wall. Knowing Silent's penchant for fire, they put together an open fire both to warm the room, and to allow him to occasionally cook something simple… maybe a potato… maybe nothing. Finally creating a door for the room, they fixed that before moving upstairs.

As the risk of accidental fires were lower here, they decided that oak walls would look nice, and started to plot out the rooms. Two large master rooms for them and Silent, three smaller guest rooms, and one crafting room. Having somewhere separate for them to turn into their work room was important, and they made sure it was a large room, with a little alcove that could maybe be a library. With the room outlines done, it didn't take them long to fill in the walls, add doors (double doors for the two master bedrooms), and move the two beds upstairs from downstairs. They decided that they should move the rest of their things up to the house from the old crafting area. With the amount of stone and wood that they had used, it only took two trips to move everything, storing it in the barrels in the kitchen. The chests that they had made were moved into the bedrooms, providing some personal storage rather than just communal ones.

Deciding to go and check on the crops and the animals, they went down the stairs, grabbing the bucket, a shovel, a hoe and the sheers just in case. Heading to the crops first, they could see that everything was ready once again for harvesting. In order to replant everything, they were going to need to expand the plot — however, despite the animals needing wheat, the potatoes were clearly of more use with each plant giving roughly three potatoes, whereas to make bread from the wheat they would need about three crops worth per loaf. Harvesting everything, they first replanted all the potatoes, having around sixty plants at this point. Leaving a strip of grass to separate the two, they started to hoe the ground to create space for about twenty plants. Ensuring that there were gaps in place for water, they finished hoeing, digging out the gaps and starting to add the water from the mini lake they made a couple of days before. Watching as the earth darkened with water, they planted twenty of the seeds for the wheat, gathered the rest and headed towards the pen that they had created for the animals. There seemed to have been a growth in numbers overnight, and Dox happily realized that they repopulated as quick as the plants seemed to grow here. Feeding them all some wheat, they sheered the sheep, gathered the wool, and headed inside, making sure to secure the gate. Unable to sit idly by and wait, they decided to create beds for the three spare rooms. Sadly, that did not take as long as they had hoped, and after placing them in the rooms, the sun had only just started to sink. Looking around at the house — well, it was more like an undecorated tavern at this point — they decided that with some of the last of the wood, they would create some tables and chairs, having somewhere for visitors to sit and eat and drink and be social. Placing the last seat down and having about ten planks of wood left over, they smiled. It was well into the night now, and the sounds had been extremely active, an explosion coming from the woods not long after they had finished with the tables. However, despite being much later than they would normally head to bed, they were extremely proud of the work that they had done. Deciding that they had completed enough work for the day, they moved to the door to double check that it was shut properly, and froze. In the distance, they heard the creak of the gate opening, followed by a snap as it was swiftly slammed shut.

Torn between getting their bow and barricading the door, or rushing out there with their sword, they cracked open the door slightly and peered out, glad of the torches lighting the area, adding visibility to the gloom. There, shuffling along towards the tavern, was Silent. They threw open the door and launched out of the doorway, hurrying to close the distance between them. Reaching him, they threw their arms around him in an almost desperate hug, his arms curling around their back just as tightly.

After a few seconds, both of them drew back, Dox's hands resting on his shoulders, studying him intently.

"Your armour looks like you tried to blow it up! *I am*

worried, what happened? Are you okay?

"Yeah, I met one of the explodey bois after the zombie orphan tried to bite my ankles. I guess all this heavy metal has *some* uses." *I am okay. Your armour saved my life. Thank you.*

"Well, you look terrible. You should get some sleep." *I am so glad you are home.*

If Silent leaned heavily on Dox while walking into the house, they didn't mention it. And if Dox left Silent's door open a little so that they could hear them if they needed to, nothing was said.

Both fell into a deep slumber, neither stirring until the following morning.

Chapter 6

When Dox awoke the next morning, they rose from the bed, wishing that they had windows to be able to look out and see what the weather was like, and somewhere to watch out for danger. Moving across the room to open the door, they took the six steps to cross the landing, inching the door to Silent's room open and looking in to see him still passed out in bed... closing the door, they headed down the stairs, knowing that Silent was probably going to be drained and would desperately need food as soon as he awoke.

They crossed to the main door, pushing it open and stepping into the weak morning sunlight. Deciding to deal with the crops first, they started to harvest and replant the potatoes, happily gathering nearly two stacks of them before moving on to the wheat, gathering the wheat and planting the seeds as they went. Having gathered everything, they moved to the animal pen, feeding the animals some of the wheat as they did. Hearing the low call from the cows, they realised that with a bucket, they could probably gather milk from them. Making a mental note to make a few buckets for this, they turned to head inside, walking straight through to the kitchen. They split the potatoes in to two stacks and placed them into the furnaces. After adding some coal to set them to cooking, they decided that they had enough wheat to make some bread; while potatoes were more filling, having some bread as a reserve would be smart. Although between the animals breeding so well and the potatoes, they should be able to thrive here. After finishing with the bread, and then storing the loaves safely within one of the chests, they moved back towards the still burning furnaces.

Checking on the potatoes, they could see that over a dozen had cooked from each of the furnaces. Pulling those that were cooked out of the furnace, they put a dozen in their personal storage container, keeping the other dozen out to give to Silent. Leaving the kitchen, they made their way up the stairs, softly knocking on Silent's door as they reached it. From within, they heard a muffled grunt that could possibly have been "come in". Smiling slightly at his typical morning grouchiness, they pushed open the door and stepped into the room.

Across the room, standing by the bed, still in full and slightly damaged armour, was Silent, still looking drained from his journey. Walking over to him, Dox lightly threw him the dozen baked potatoes. With visible relief, Silent quickly devoured the first one, seeming to move with a little more energy as soon as he had finished it. The next three disappeared almost as quickly as the first before he stored the other eight for when he next needed them. Green eyes brightening as his hunger was finally sated, he smiled at Dox.

"Okay, so what is the plan for today?"

"Well, as you seem to be doing well after some food, I thought we could sit down in the kitchen, have a catch-up on what we have done over the last couple of days, and make a plan for the next few days? Maybe fix a couple of things here, but stay close to home for the day?"

"Oh, fix things like the wonky gate?" The fond smile he threw their way took any sting out of the comment, making Dox grin in return.

"I was thinking more like the damage to perfectly good

armour!"

Falling back into the easy banter of family let the final ache of tension fall from both of their shoulders, safe in the knowledge that they were back together again.

"Oh, and new rule of home! No armour in the house."

"Wait, what? No, you made this for me, I'm not just going to take it off every time I walk through the door!"

Dox fixed Silent with a steely eyed gaze, their purple eyes flashing with a challenge.

"You know what, you are absolutely right! Armour should absolutely not be worn in the house!" he said. Already pulling off his armour, he stored it in his personal storage. It took up four places as the types of equipment were different.

Turning to hide their grin, Dox walked out of the room, heading for the stairs.

Following Dox out of the room, Silent took the time to actually look around at the house, marvelling at the size and the detailing that had gone into this in such a short space of time. Dox really can build anything that they want to! Crossing the landing, they peaked through the other set of double doors into the room opposite, correctly assuming that it was Dox's. Seeing other doors further away from the stairs, he walked over to investigate. Opening the next three single doors revealed sparsely decorated rooms, with nothing more than a bed. The last two rooms were completely empty, what would be in them a mystery to all but Dox.

Wandering back along the hall to the stairs, he was once again impressed by the amount that Dox had completed, well aware that Dox was probably already working on plans A to at least M of what needed to be done, changed, or created. Following the stairs as they curved down, he reached the ground floor and seemed to be standing in a dining area, tables and chairs dotted around, with what looked like a bar opposite them. Hearing Dox from behind the other door in the room, he called out.

"Hey, Dox — with the number of rooms and tables and chairs in here, are you planning on adopting everyone we meet?"

He practically heard them roll their eyes as he walked towards the door.

"Thought we could have a bit of a tavern or way station, either to help people who are new here like us — and they can owe us favours like mining for us — or people can pay for food or to stay here."

"Umm, Dox Darling, you getting people to mine for us kind of sounds like slave labour there?"

"Noooo that's not what I meant! I didn't mean it like that! Just that we might agree to give them food or stuff, or a place to stay, and when they are on their feet, they could give us a specific amount of iron or coal or something."

Grinning at the flustered tone in their voice, Silent pushed the door open to reveal a kitchen, two furnaces burning, and plenty of storage, but most importantly, a fire pit! The frustrated glare Dox gave him at the grin was ruined by the slight upturn of their mouth. As Dox moved towards him, he let them shoo him back out the door and towards the closest chair. Sitting down, he watched them move around the table to sit on the other side.

"Okay Silent, you can see what I have been working on. What happened on your travels?"

For the next few hours, Silent spoke, talking about the start of his journey and briefly mentioning that he had met a rude merchant in the woods, before rapidly changing the subject to talk about the flower fields that he had found. Passing over the eggs that he had found, he moved on to talk about seeing a village in the distance and the birch woods, finding the sheep, and being about to make a rudimentary portable bed from one of Dox's past designs, making sleeping a lot more comfortable. Trying to explain a pitch-black creature that can teleport, and make someone believe you, is harder than it seems. And while Dox didn't call him a liar or anything like that, he could see the scepticism in their eyes. Moving on to the disgusting trek through the swamp and finding a hole in the ground to sleep in, he completely ignored his nightmare, just mentioning that he had decided that it was time to head home. By the time his storytelling was done, a few hours had passed. Shifting slightly and sitting up straighter in their seat, Dox made eye contact with Silent.

"Wow, okay, that is a lot to take in there. But quick question; what happened with the merchant and the llamas?"

"We just had a mild disagreement. On a completely unrelated note, I managed to find some leather and leads on my travels."

"Hmmm sure, completely unrelated note, I am so convinced! This is why I didn't want you to go into any villages!"

With an offended huff, Silent changed the subject, not exactly having a defence right now.

"So, what still needs doing here? The house is looking good."

"Well at some point we need to put in some decoration and things, but it is structurally good, and functioning. Mainly we need to get a stockpile of food, coal, iron and other things. I also want to go to the village and work out if there is anything that they trade in that we have, or that we can't easily get and can trade for."

"So, mining, farming, and then a visit to the village?"

"Yee that sounds good to me. Village tomorrow? Or the day after?"

"Well, I found an actual mine down there, so maybe farming for the next hour or so, then head down to the mine with a couple of spare beds and explore and mine this afternoon/evening and tomorrow? Good night's rest at the tavern and then take some things with us to trade at the village?"

"Bet."

Both standing, Dox moved to the front double doors, Silent trailing behind them. Taking his first step outside, Silent had his first proper look of the farm in the daylight. Gone was the makeshift shed that they stayed in for their first nights, and the makeshift crafting area with the chests. A large farm with wheat and potatoes was to one side, with an irrigation-type system, and to the other side was a large pen with cows and sheep.

Taking a deep breath of fresh air, Silent started towards the crops, a bounce in his step. Reaching the first potato crop, he plucked it from the ground, gaining four potatoes, and quickly replanting one of them in the hoed ground. Repeating the action, he could see Dox doing the same with the wheat, replanting the seeds from the wheat as they went. Finishing the first row he turned to continue the next, repeating until there was only a sea of small green shoots of new potato plants. Seeing that Dox was nearly finished on their side, he headed back into the house to start cooking them. Speeding through the double doors and crossing to the single door, he headed straight to the furnace before freezing. Turning around, he stared at the fire pit. A grin on his face, he placed potatoes around the edge of the pit to cook, gazing into the flames and swapping the cooked potatoes with the raw ones when he could.

Having finished replanting the wheat, Dox saw Silent enter

the house, assuming that he had gone in to set the potatoes cooking. Dox headed over to the animals. Quickly feeding all of the animals, Dox did a quick head count of them. They now had fourteen cows and twenty sheep. Spending a few minutes out there, just enjoying the sounds of the animals, they heard the distinctive *oink* of a pig. Turning to look, they could see that there were some pigs standing outside the fence. Still holding some of the wheat, they headed over to the gate, opened it, and walked round to where the pigs were. Offering them some of the wheat and backing away towards the gate, they were disappointed when the pigs barely even glanced in their direction. Trying again, they were ignored once more. With a huff of disappointment, they put the wheat away, and ran back to the gate. Sweeping their gaze across their claimed land, there was no sign of Silent, so they headed to the front door. Entering the tavern and moving to the kitchen door, they pushed the door open and stopped. There, standing in the middle of the room, staring into the fire, a vacant look on his face, was Silent. He didn't react to Dox entering the room, when they crossed the room to the chests, or even them opening and closing the chests to store the wheat. There was only the mechanical movement of Dox swapping over the potatoes when they deemed that they were cooked. Sighing, Dox turned to face Silent fully.

"And this is why I don't leave you alone to cook!"

Jumping and spinning around Silent stared at Dox with wild eyes, heart racing to the point that his pulse was visible in his neck.

"Oh… hey Dox, been here long?"

Just letting out a small laugh, Dox took the stack of potatoes that Silent hadn't managed to cook yet and placed them in the furnace, taking out the cooked ones that had finished cooking from earlier. Having about a stack and a half cooked, with Silent admitting to having about the same, Dox stored the ones that they had and took half of the ones that Silent had.

With Silent still pouting slightly about being stopped from playing with fire, they started to collect what they would need for exploring the cave. Taking two iron pickaxes each from the ones made days earlier, Dox also grabbed their armour to put on down in the caves, as well as their sword, shield and bow. They then headed upstairs to adjust one of the spare beds into a portable one to take with them, knowing that Silent already had his.

Checking his own inventory, Silent remembered the sugar cane that he had picked up. Not wanting to distract Dox, he stored it in one of the chests along with the flowers. Ensuring that he had both his armour and diamond sword, he picked up the two pickaxes that Dox had left for him, before heading to one of the chests to grab a few more torches. Upon opening the chest, he saw the diamond pickaxe that Dox said they were going to make for him as he left before. Grabbing it with a smile, he quickly stored it.

Chapter 7

Once Dox had returned, the two of them headed out the front door and towards the tunnel leading down to the mines. Making quick work of the steps, which were thankfully lit up by torches already, and starting to hear faint noises, they soon came to the blockage that Silent had made at the end to prevent anything following him out. The sounds had started to get somewhat louder, and they were clearly able to hear the rattle of the skeletons, the groaning of a zombie, and the hissing of the spiders. Making sure that they both had their shields on and easy reach of their swords, Silent used his pickaxe to break through the final two blocks to the mine.

Dox was shocked by the mine; with the wooden platforms that stretched above open caverns and through into tunnels, there was clearly a lot of work that had gone on to put this together. Following Silent, they had a non-verbal agreement to stick together as Silent explained that he had placed the torches on the left-hand side of the wall so that to get home, he would just have to follow them back with them on his right. Seeing the logic in this, Dox turned to follow the torches that showed the route Silent had started to explore. As they rounded the corner to where Silent had found the chest, they ran into a skeleton.

Immediately spotting them, it drew back its bow to fire. Dox swapped from sword to bow and fired, hitting the skeleton. As it fired back, Silent took its first arrow on his shield. Running at the now injured skeleton, one hit from his diamond sword was all that was needed for it to be dispatched. Gathering the bones, arrows and bow that it left behind, he passed them to Dox, who noticed that on that last shot, there was some damage to the bow string. As the one just dropped had a perfectly good string, they quickly combined the two to replace it.

Keeping their bow out, Silent swapped from sword to torches, and as they continued exploring, he placed torches down on the left. Finding an exposed vein of both gold and iron on opposite sides of the tunnel, they swapped their weapons for their pickaxes, Silent sticking with an iron one, and got to work. Quickly mining into either wall, Silent soon had seven gold ore and Dox had twelve iron ore. Deciding that having a little bit of cobblestone on them would be a good idea, they both mined half a dozen blocks to store. Realising that they had mined the section that held the torch, Dox picked it up and moved it slightly further along the wall. No more than twenty steps further, there was a large patch of coal on the right. Mining from either side, they quickly fell into a routine, mining, placing torches, and killing the occasional monster that attacked them. They both quickly became adapt at swapping between torch and pickaxe to their weapons.

The first time they came to a junction, they followed the left side passage down some steps, finding some more iron ore and coal and a dead end. Heading back up the steps after collecting the ore, they took the torches with them, and used some of the additional cobblestone that they had to block up the passage. Continuing along the main path, only veering off for paths that were dead ends, they cleared the ores and blocked them up. Hitting the end of where they could go straight, they agreed to go left at the end and repeat.

Rounding the corner to the left, Silent jumped back at the

zombie in front of them, crashing into Dox.

"It has a weapon!"

"It's a spoon!"

It was a shovel… as the zombie shambled towards them brandishing its shovel, Silent jumped forwards to attack as Dox nocked and loosed an arrow, hitting the zombie just as Silent got close enough to attack. It ignored him, aiming towards Dox with the shovel. Loading another arrow, they shot again as Silent attacked from behind. Realizing that he was hitting it with a lump of iron ore, he swapped back to his sword, and hit it a third time, watching it crumble to a lump of rotten flesh.

Breathing heavily, they looked at each other.

"A spoon?" asked Silent, before laughter took over. Each pulling out a potato to eat, and feeling a little fatigued, they continued along the mine shaft. Deciding that it was probably time to get some sleep, they dug into the wall, creating an alcove that they added torches to before blocking themselves in. Laying out the portable beds side by side, they settled in to get some sleep. After so long spent on the road together, whether they could see the sun or not, they both had an internal body clock that rarely steered them wrong. Laying down in bed, with the amount of work they had done, sleep claimed them quickly. Feeling completely rested, they both started to stir, and neither enjoying lying in bed once they were up, they were quickly up and moving. They decided that they would leave the beds where they were, in case they overestimated the amount of time they spent and needed to rest on their way back.

Digging through the wall they made, they headed back along the mine. Before long, they came to a large area, a little more open with a crossroads. In the middle of it was a chest. Opening the chest, there was a leather saddle, some iron horse armour, four more diamonds and some seeds. As the chest closed, from the left-hand path they heard the scuttle of spiders. Looking up, a spider appeared, but not the normal black ones; this one was a blue-green colour and seemed to move slightly faster as it ran towards them.

Dox's first arrow missed, and Silent stepped in front of them swinging with the diamond sword. Although he hit it, the spider got past the shield and bit him, causing him to stumble back. Dox managed to set off another arrow which was successful. Two more arrows and a solid hit from Silent, and the spider was nothing more than an eye and some string. Panting, a shiver wracked Silent as the poison from the spider coursed through his body. Feeling severe fatigue settle in, he put his sword away and shakily reached for one of the potatoes. As he dug into his food, Dox hovered in concern, knowing from past experience that if one of them became too injured, the only thing they could do was drop everything and crawl back to their bed. Luckily, with two of them, most of the stuff could be picked up by the other, but it was not nice to witness, or to happen to them. As Silent ate, the shaking stopped, and the dull tint that had crept into his eyes began to recede.

"Okay, I vote that we follow to the end of this path, and then head back?" said Dox.

Still getting over the feeling of the poison in his body, Silent just nodded. Shaking off the final feelings of the poison, Silent started along the mine shaft, but Dox didn't follow, making him pause.

Quickly pulling out some of the cobblestone, they put together a wall, blocking that entrance from allowing any poisonous spiders to come hunting for them. Now with Dox by his side, they continued the way they had been going, mining everything that they could. Reaching the end of the mineshaft, they could see that it dipped down into extremely uneven stairs, followed by a drop.

"Head down and have a look before we head back?" asked Silent.

"If you are up for it?!" replied Dox.

Without answering, Silent took a few steps back and started mining into the rock, creating a staircase down. Running out of rock to mine before they could reach the ground, Silent crouched down on the lowest step, reaching as far and as low as he could, and managed to place a block on the wall opposite, a bit lower than he currently was. Adding on to the front of it, one above that, one in front, and one above, he reached the step that he was on, and was able to make his way to the wall and therefore able to lean down, place a block below, step down onto it, and repeat. Eventually, they had a crude staircase leading to the bottom of the ravine. Placing a torch, Dox noticed that there seemed to be light coming from ahead, along with a hissing, popping sound. As the duo walked forwards, getting closer to the light source, they started to feel the temperature heat up. Looking slightly up, Dox nudged Silent, pointing at the waterfall of lava pouring from a rock above them. Walking a little further up, they could hear the rushing of water, and as they reached what could only be described as a lake of lava, they could see a waterfall on the far side. The two elements had clashed to form a black rock. Unable to see a way past, they agreed to mine the area that they could easily reach before retuning another time.

Splitting up, they each took a side of the ravine, mining everything they could. On the last patch of iron, the pickaxe that Dox had been using shattered in their grip. About to turn around to head back to the stairs, they saw a glimmer of blue. Excited, they shouted for Silent, who ran over, jumping slightly for speed as he did.

"My pickaxe just broke, but I think that this might be diamond!"

Swapping over to his diamond pickaxe, noting how damaged his second iron one was, Silent carefully mined, grinning when he was rewarded with not only a diamond, but another in the space below and behind it. Continuing to mine, they were thrilled when in total, they had eight diamonds from this area. Digging into the blocks a little bit each side to make sure nothing was missed, they moved back, happy with the total of twelve diamonds that they had.

"I think we have got as much as we are going to today. Let's head home."

Agreeing, Silent turned back towards the stairs, only to yelp as a skeleton fell from a ledge above them, landing painfully. Raising his shield to catch the first arrow, they both switched to their weapons. Dox's arrow hit first, closely followed by Silent's sword, and the skeleton crumbled.

Heart rate returning to normal, they headed to the stairs. Making their way up, they followed their path back, keeping the torches to their right. They stopped only to deal with the few monsters that attacked them and to collect their beds.

Reaching the bottom of the staircase that would lead them home, they crossed over, with Silent once again sealing the entrance behind them. The last thing they wanted was those spiders finding their way up into their house. Reaching the top of the steps and finally stepping into the cool air and the dim light of sunset felt amazing. But being able to walk to the tavern, call it home and set two stacks of iron in the furnaces felt even better. Just the notion of having a home, one that they were thriving in, was amazing. Though they would never say it out loud, they both felt a sense of security there, knowing that they had somewhere that was theirs, and they made it. With so much iron and gold that needed to be smelted, they were lucky that they had found more than enough coal. Amazingly, they had managed to bring up just over two stacks of iron, a stack of gold and twelve diamonds. To go with that, there were several stacks of coal between them. Extremely happy with the work that they had done in the past few days, they sat down after removing their armour, looking forward to the break before they travelled to the village the next day. Keeping half an eye on the furnace and swapping the ores over as they smelted, they fell into a comfortable silence, enjoying the peace of the evening. Suddenly remembering the sugarcane, Silent went over to the chest and pulled it out. Walking back to Dox, he explained that he had found it growing on the edge of the water and thought that it might be worth attempting to plant some by the pond. Agreeing, they left the warm comfort of the kitchen and headed through the tavern and outside. Walking towards the pond, it was easy to plant, making sure it was directly against the water.

"We could probably use that to make paper if we needed it, for maps or books or something."

Humming in agreement, Silent led the way back inside. A few hours later, after swapping the smelted iron with the gold, and once again repeating the process, they headed upstairs. Separating on the landing, they moved across to open the doors to their respective rooms. Getting into bed, and closing his eyes, Silent tried to find sleep, but it did not immediately come as it had in previous nights since they had been in this place. Instead, they listened to Dox as they moved about their room, opening and closing their chest as they put things away. Hearing them get into bed, Silent's eyes became heavy, slipping swiftly into a deep slumber.

Chapter 8

Waking up the next morning, Dox could feel the excitement brewing at the fact that they would be going to the village! Springing out of bed, they moved across to the chest that they had placed in their room. Opening it, they grabbed the iron, gold, and diamonds that they had stored in there and made their way downstairs. They could hear Silent moving around upstairs, and knew that he would soon join them. While waiting for him, Dox decided to try and make the bits that they would need for the foreseeable future, so that they could take the rest to try and trade.

Entering the kitchen, they moved to the crafting table, and quickly put together two sets of armour, knowing that with the damage that Silent had already done to his, it would be a good idea to have spare. Moving them to a chest, they could see that they did not have any spare wood. Grabbing the slightly damaged axe that Silent had been using, they bounded through the tavern and out the door. Speeding across to the fence, they pushed the wonky creaking gate open and headed to the woods. Moving to the closest large tree, they cut off one of the branches, gaining enough wood for twelve planks. Heading back into the house and making sure the gate and the door were securely closed, they headed straight for the crafting table, stripping the logs down into planks and then breaking them down to twenty-four sticks. Grabbing two of the diamonds, they made a second diamond sword, knowing that Silent would want them to have it available if they needed it. Using the rest of the sticks, they made a combination of axes and pickaxes, storing them in the chest. As they closed the chest, they heard Silent walking across the floor, followed by the front door closing. Had he been outside?

As he pushed the door open, Dox smiled at the raw potatoes that he was holding, letting him spread some around the fire before taking the others to put in the furnace to cook. Ignoring his pout, Dox stepped around him, handing him twenty cooked potatoes.

"You got everything that you need for this trip to the village?"

"I have made some things for us out of the iron, and have stored them. I have also packed up all of the other resources to take with us."

"Ahh, I am guessing that you used the wood for that?"

"Mhmm… wait, were you outside?"

He rolled his eyes at how oblivious they were when they were focused on something.

"Yes, I was doing some farming and you ran right past me."

"Oh, okay then. Anyway, I have everything and am ready to go."

Walking to the door, Silent pulled on his armour as he went. Leaving the tavern and starting to cross to the gate, Silent looked at Dox.

"You gonna put on your armour, Dox?"

"Ummm, sure, let me just go check… something real quick."

And with that, they ran back into the tavern, disappearing towards the stairs. Silent shook his head, knowing that their armour would probably still be in a chest in their room.

Waiting and watching the door, he thought back to their first meetings.

After gathering everything he would need, Silent donned his usual reinforced leather clothing, and a red cloak to keep him warm, and to replicate the weight that was missing from his back. He headed to the southern edge of the village, where he had agreed to meet Dox. A strange feeling fluttered in his stomach; would they show up?

In all honesty, he didn't know what prompted him to make that offer. There was never many of his kind, no one who even knew what "his kind" meant, what or who they were. All he knew was that they were creatures of air and fire, his earliest memories being of flames, a bright slash of colour in an otherwise dark place. Dark rock surrounding him, he used the light of the flames to navigate. The first time he pushed away from the earth, the warm currents of air from the flames caught under the wings, rising him higher. Looking up, he tilted his shoulders up, causing him to gain more height, and then tilted to the left to spiral upwards, gazing into the infinite dark above... and then he looked down! Below him, sparkly specks of light pushed back the dark, creating patterns and swirls. He faltered in mid-air at the beauty below. Stilling his wings and gliding, he was just entranced by the fire, the way the flames danced and sparks flew. His first memory of flight was also the first time he met someone like him. After reaching a higher thermal, he had caught a flash of colour at his level. Seeing the speck spiral down to the ground, he followed. Speeding towards the ground, he braced his wings and braked sharply, becoming vertical and allowing his feet to softly touch the ground. Walking closer to the other being, he took in their form; wings that gently brushing the ground, tall frame, and broad shoulders. Stumbling slightly, more uncoordinated with his feet on solid ground, he kicked a rock, causing it to scatter over the ground. Head jerking up, the other being stared at him with startled eyes before opening its wings and jumping to the sky, fleeing into the darkness.

Blinking back to the path he was walking down, he brushed his fingers over the thick red material of the cloak. While the material did nothing to fill the whole in his soul, it did assist him with his balance. While flying had been a natural thing for him, learning to be on the ground was harder. Gangly limbs were easy to trip over, and after you face plant the floor one too many times, it is easier to remain in the air. After his loss, he accepted that he would never again meet one of his kind, unlikely to ever see them on the ground. He therefore spent so many years alone, closed off and cold, unable and unwilling to emotionally connect with anyone, solid in his belief that no one else could understand the emotional loss.

And then he met his Paradox. Someone so willing to help him, but with such raw pain searing from their eyes. A burning loneliness that he could almost touch like an aura around them, but also a sense of calm and peace. After leaving them that first day, he had walked to the edge of the village, and crossed the border, ready to leave and never look back — after all, the job was done, and there was no need to stick around. Heading down an animal trail off the beaten path, he was ready to lose himself in the woods, maybe spend a couple of weeks off the grid and away from everyone. Less than half an hour later, a feeling of loss brought him to his knees, the feeling of a lost opportunity flowing through him in waves. A pair of purple eyes filled his mind, a tug of the first connection that he hadn't felt in years, and without conscious thought, he pulled himself up, turned back to the village and started back. He found himself on the edge of the village with very little memory of how he got there. He stared into the small crowd of people moving around each other like sheep, their appearances so different from each other, but with herd mentality. No one moving from the crowd, they all just fitted into the dull world of grey. A bright spot weaved through the crowd, avoiding physical contact with all that they passed, moving within the crowd, but seeming separate. His eyes followed his Paradox, watching to see as they entered a shop. He moved towards the buildings, getting closer to the door that they had disappeared into. Glancing into the window by the door, squinting into the darkness, there were various devices sitting on shelves that cluttered the walls. A long work bench took up the far wall, standing next to a rundown and slightly wonky door. The room that was visible was empty, but there was a rumble of voices filtering from beyond the door. Unwilling to ask anyone, he started to analyse the objects on the walls, seeing some things that looked in need of repair and some that looked to be newly made. Looking to the work bench, he could see half created objects with sketches and plans on paper scattered around. He realised that the shop was either some type of repair shop, a shop dedicated to creating or improving things, or a combination of the two. Moving away from the window, he re-joined the crowd, heading towards what seemed to be a town square. At the centre was a large water fountain with a large stone half moon rising above it. Stepping onto the ledge of the water fountain, he got a hold of the bottom of the half moon and pulled up, using momentum and light body weight to launch up, grab the top of the moon, and swing up to perch on the top. Crouching on the ball of his feet, it was the perfect vantage point to watch the crowd. Enjoying watching people's reactions to him, he estimated the number of people that did not notice him getting down — those that noticed immediately, he viewed as slightly more of a threat. As he sat there, people watching, he began to make a plan to get close to Paradox again. If they worked within the shop, and

75

created things, Silent would ask for something new to be created; if they fixed things, he would need something broken to bring in, and if they just built things that already existed, then he would think of something that needed making. The last would be easy; a pocket watch would be a useful thing to have. But the other two would require a little more thought. Listening to the murmur from the crowd, he shifted the small pack that sat under his cloak; it small for convenience, but unable to carry everything that could be useful. That would be an idea! A pack that was small enough to carry, but could fit so much more in it! So that was one and three sorted. He didn't really have anything that was broken, though. Having a small pack didn't really allow him to keep things for sentimental reasons. Something small like a broken clock or music box would be good. During his musings, he didn't notice that the sun had started to set, and the crowd had thinned out to just the occasional straggler as people returned to their homes. Staying where he was until full dark, he waited for the lights in the houses to turn off. Hundreds of sleepless nights had led to this, having lost the need or desire to sleep until his body was ready to shut down, preferring instead to lay in the dark, process the day, and relax. When the last light was extinguished, he swung down from the moon, cape fluttering to settle heavily around him. Wandering through the empty streets, an evil thought occurred to him. Making his way to the slightly larger houses at the outskirts, he started to peer into the windows. Finding a house that had a smallish clock above the fireplace, he backtracked towards the door, removed a knife from his belt, and dug it into the gap between the slightly rotten wooden door and the stone wall. Glad that the door was poorly made, he was able to use the knife to knock out the latch and open the door. Pushing it slowly open, he crept through into the front room, grabbed the clock, and rapidly exited, pulling the door quietly closed and stowing the clock into his bag. Moving further from the edge of the village, he found a barn. He scrambled up into the hayloft and settled against the hay to rest for the remainder of the night, set on heading to the store the next day.

As Dox left the tavern, now wearing full armour, Silent pulled himself back to the present and gave a small nod as they drew level, turning to move out of the gate. Setting off at a bouncing sprint, they enjoyed the freedom of being able to stretch their legs and let loose. Heading into the woods and following the faint light of torches, they enjoyed the wind in their faces as the trees sped through. Moving like this was so familiar that they could forget where they were, effortlessly moving around each other and springing over falling branches and the occasional random rock. Weaving around trees, hands occasionally brushing, they were constantly aware of the other as the miles slipped away. The oak trees started to thin out, with a few flowers starting to crop up. Ignoring the terrain change, they sped on; Silent knowing that the village would be just over the next hill, and Dox because they would follow Silent wherever he led.

In the distance, Dox could see the tip of a roof, and less than a minute later, the terrain changed again, showing them a path. Slowing to a walk, they both pulled out a potato, knowing from past experience that there wasn't always a warm welcome for strangers in villages. Walking along the path, the outline of houses was becoming clearer.

"Does it seem odd to you that there are no fences? Especially with the number of monsters here."

"Actually, yes. I didn't think of it when I passed originally, but you're right."

"We will have to ask them. So, are you going to stick by me

77

and not talk to the nice villagers, or are you going to wait by the edge?"

"Wow, what do you think I am going to do? Just go round stabbin' people if you leave me unsupervised?"

"Yes!"

"Okay that's fair, but I will be on my best behaviour and stay by you."

Reaching the edge of the first house, they saw the reason that there was no need for a fence. A huge mountain of a being walked past them, and by the looks of it, it was entirely created from iron. Turning to face them and stepping into their path, the creature stopped and stared at them.

Chapter 9

The intimidation of such a large and solid creature had Silent loosening his sword, ready to defend them if needed, but without appearing threatening. With a slow steady pace, however, the creature turned back towards the village and walked away. Letting out a small breath, the pair continued on, passing the first houses and entering what looked to be a town square. There were some small stalls set up, a golden bell hanging above them. Villagers moved around with purpose, each wearing something that seemed to reflect their trade.

Having the most experience dealing with people who created things, Dox headed first for a house that had a large furnace, and someone wearing a heavy leather apron. Correctly assuming that they were an armourer, they struck up a conversation. The male was unwilling to give up his name, however was more than happy to advise that as a village, they traded in emeralds. He explained that there were many different merchants here, like a librarian who trades in enchanted books which could be used to enhance things like armour and weapons, and who will happily buy paper to assist them in creating the books. A cleric, who trades in things like enchanting potions to assist you in combining enchantments with things and who wants to buy things like gold and the rotten flesh of zombies. There were farmers who bought things like wheat and potatoes and would sell things like bread and pie. A fletcher who wanted sticks and feathers but would sell arrows. If you wanted maps, there was also a cartographer who would sell them to you, and would also buy paper if you had it. Finally, the man himself advised that he was an armourer, and sold everything from iron armour to enchanted diamond armour, but would always be happy to buy things like iron, coal, flint and diamonds. He said that there were other trades in other villages if anything different was wanted.

Ecstatic, Dox was practically bouncing in place. Already pulling out the iron and coal that they had to trade, the man explained that for fifteen coal, or four iron, he would give one emerald. Doing the math, they worked out that for the coal they had brought with them, they would gain eight emeralds, and after quickly making the exchange, Dox looked at the amount of iron they had; having brought 116 ingots with them, they could get twenty-nine emerald. Sadly however, the armourer only had seventeen emeralds that they were able to trade with for the iron, but said that after they had used some and made some sales, they would be happy to trade again. Walking away from the armourer twenty-five emeralds richer, Dox was keen to speak to someone else.

"Hey, look over by the bell, there is someone in a purple tunic thing," said Silent.

Looking to where Silent had indicated, Dox changed route, heading to them.

Reaching where they were standing, Dox was quick to start up a conversation with them. Once again unwilling to give a name, they told Dox that they worked as a cleric. As Dox explained that they were new to the area, the cleric was happy to talk about some of the weird and wonderful things that they trade in. The first thing they mentioned was Redstone, which Silent recognised as something that he had mined during his first expedition. The cleric advised that you could use it to create automated devices that would function alone, such as a compass or a clock or various pistons. Excited to experiment with it when they got home, Dox moved the conversation on to other things that the cleric traded in. There were a few specific plants that only grew in places that you could get to through a portal, things that were made from the hardest of materials, found when lava is quickly cooled by water, and only able to be mined if you had a diamond pickaxe. Anything less, and *if* you managed to mine it, then it would be too damaged and crumble. While the cleric had not personally crossed over through a portal, they were able to describe a couple of the broken portals that they had seen, waiting for someone to patch them and relight them. The pair were told about the different dangers in this other world, full of lava and floating creatures that shot fire from their mouths. Halfway through the cleric's description of the natives — strange creatures with an obsession with gold, who would remain friendly if you were wearing some kind of golden armour to distract them — Silent's eyes dimmed, and he turned abruptly, running from the village. Finishing their conversation, Dox was quick to trade with the cleric, managing to gain eighteen emeralds from the gold that they had carried with them.

Moving away from the cleric, Dox scanned the area, hoping to be able to spot Silent. Unable to see him, they moved to the edge of the village in case they could see him. No sign of the man remained. A ball of panic started to form within their stomach, growing larger and starting to move up. The crushing pressure hit their lungs caused them to gasp for air, vision blurring from unshed tears as the long-forgotten feeling of loneliness swept through them. He had never left like this, even when they had argued, or when he had gone wandering, he always told them, always said goodbye.

81

Trying to force down the panic, they looked out into the surrounding area, realising that at some point they had fallen to their knees. Trying to gather some semblance of control, they focused on the fact that Silent wouldn't just leave without a good reason. Maybe he was struggling with the urge to stab something and couldn't verbalise it, so went for a run. Yes, that was probably it. He would be back. They just needed to carry on gathering information from the villagers and he would be back. Wiping away the tears that had started to escape from their eyes, they stood. Turning back to the village, they pushed back the feeling of abandonment and the reminder that everyone that they had ever loved before Silent had left them. Silent wouldn't do that! They were a pair! Platonically married. He would not just leave.

Moving back into the village, they could see a slightly larger building to the far side and headed that way. Pushing open the door, they were excited to see that it was a library. After hearing about magical books from the Armourer, they were excited to learn more. Peering around the room, they spotted the Librarian standing by a tall wooden desk. Moving over to them, they were quick to jump into a conversation about the way books were enchanted, listening intently as she described a table with a floating book, which needed to be made using diamonds, obsidian, and a book, and how there was a dark blue stone that they called lapis that could be used to add enchantments to objects, and that they could be used to create enchanted books, which could be saved to enchant objects at a later date. Eager to absorb as much information as they could, Dox asked about how to combine the book with the item they might want to enchant. Sketching out an iron anvil to create gave them something new to focus on. With enough iron, they could make this; they would just have to get Silent to go mining... the thought of Silent hit like a punch to the gut, but focusing on the Librarian, they asked what enchanted books they sold. She told them that they could enchant a book with Mending, which would cause the item to take energy from mining things like coal or Redstone which gave off a certain energy, or energy that was given when killing things like the zombies or skeletons. Sadly, Dox did not have a book with them, or the means to make one right now, although they promised to return when they did.

Leaving the Librarian, they headed back to the town square, unsure what to do now. They had plenty of food, and they could make the armour and weapons and enjoyed doing it. They were looking forwards to experimenting with the Redstone, and also to finding and mending one of the portals, although if it was as dangerous as the Librarian said, maybe they would use the ten diamonds they had left to make a chest plate. They had enough gold to make golden helmets for both them and Silent, but they would feel better if at least Silent was in a full set of stronger armour. Actually, they had forty-three emeralds, and the armourer that they were talking to earlier sold some enchanted diamond armour. Unsure how much they would cost, they headed back over to the man, establishing that the boots and helmet were thirteen diamonds each, the leggings nineteen, and the chest plate twenty-one. Sadly, they would not have enough to buy a full set, but they could buy Silent the leggings and the chest plate, and then make gold boots and diamond helmets for them both. That would mean that they were as protected as possible, with Silent being more invested in close quarters fighting. Agreeing to the trade and taking the items, they made their way to the outskirts of the village, unsure whether they should leave or not. A flicker of movement heading their way answered that question.

Hearing about the gold-obsessed creatures from another place caused a fiery rage to burn through Silent, and forcing himself to shut down slightly, he turned from the cleric and ran. He did not want his Paradox to see him lose control, not like this. The level of bloodlust that he could feel rising in him was not something they needed to witness. The story of his loss is not one that they fully knew, only knowing that his wings were taken from him after he had made a mistake. They did not need the images that the full story would give to them. They deserved better than that horror.

They had seen him at his lowest, when the darkness crept into his mind, and they had comforted him with their very presence. But the monster locked within him was something that might cause them fear, and he would never knowingly do that to them. While they knew he was far from innocent, and an assassin on occasion, knowing and seeing were two very different things. Hitting the edge of the village, Silent did not slow down, and his ears pricked for any sound. Finally, he heard it, a low *moo* to his left, and he turned, quickly spotting the cow. Heading towards it, he could see that it was in a small herd of seven or eight cows. Taking out his sword, he swung, felling the first with two blows. Mind fogged in red, his next movements were a blur, unaware of time or his surroundings. Slowing to a stop and breathing harshly, bloodlust sated, the fog cleared. Looking around him, there was no longer anything alive; the cows were gone, along with a couple of sheep that he hadn't noticed to start with.

Letting out a sigh, he gathered up what he could, not believing in waste. The leather could be used to cover books, and the meat is always useful. The wool from the sheep could be used for spare beds if nothing else.

Taking a few breaths, calm once again, he realized that in his red fogged brain, he had abandoned Dox at the village for who knows how long. Turning back, he started back towards the village, picking up speed as he did so.

Meeting Dox at the edge of the village, guilt crept in as he saw them visibly relax, forcibly reminding him that they were once abandoned by their entire family. Moving as close to them as possible, he handed over the leather, meat and wool. A peace offering.

Taking it from him, Dox explained that there was not really anyone else that they wanted to speak to or trade with. Looking at the time, and knowing that they were not going to make it back to the tavern before dark, Silent suggested that they set up their spare beds in one of the empty houses and head off in the morning. Looking at the slowly darkening sky, they agreed, moving towards a vacant house and laying out their beds. Before getting into bed, Dox updated Silent on what he had missed, pointing out the library through the window. By the time that they had finished explaining everything, it was full dark, and the rest of the village was asleep. Laying down, Dox closed their eyes, but hearing Silent moving around kept sleep from them, and hearing him softly leave through the door tore all ideas of sleep away.

Silent left the little hut, intent on having a look around the village with a little more privacy. Heading to the library first, he dismantled one of the bookshelves, being left with a few books that he had gathered. Deciding that you could never have too many books, he moved throughout the room, dismantling all of the bookshelves, and ended up with thirty books from the ten shelves he had destroyed. Looking around, there was nothing else of interest there, and they moved on to the next house, finding a chest that held a saddle and some carrots, which he quickly scooped up. Continuing to move around the village, he gathered a few pieces of paper, some emerald, a couple of empty glass bottles and another saddle. Creeping back into the hut that they were staying in, they were met, not by a bed and a sleeping Dox, but instead a wide awake, angry-eyed Dox standing in the doorway.

"Ah, I can explain?"

"Okay?"

"Listen…"

"…"

"I just wanted to explore a bit?"

"Are you asking me or telling me?"

"Telling?"

Dox sighed. "Just go to bed! No more late-night pilfering please."

"I… you know me too well."

Scuttling around Dox, Silent quickly got into his bed, deciding to do as he was told for once and closing his eyes quickly, hearing Dox do the same. They both quickly drifted off to sleep.

Chapter 10

Awakening to the sun creeping through the window, both agreed that after Silent's late night adventure, they would probably be better off leaving quickly. So, after packing up the beds, they exited the hut and headed back towards home. Looking at Dox, Silent could see that they were still struggling slightly with him leaving the night before. They didn't have to say anything; it was telegraphed throughout their body, in the stiffness in their shoulders and the dull look in their eyes. Guilt-ridden at the pain that they had caused the most important person in his life, Silent took a deep breath to steady himself.

"I probably owe you an explanation for yesterday. I — you know a little about the day I lost my wings?"

"You don't need to explain. I know you don't like to talk about that, and I get it. It is okay."

Almost grabbing the escape that they were offering, Silent closed his eyes, hiding the pain that flared up in the depths of green.

"No, it isn't okay, Dox. I…"

Dox physically putting their hand over his mouth stopped him mid-sentence, shocking him with the casual touch. As close as they were, physical touch wasn't massively common for them. Looking at them, confused, Dox elaborated.

"I am guessing it had something to do with a subject that we have a mutual agreement not to talk about. And I am outright stating, that right now, I do not want to know. I trust you, and I know who you are now, and that is enough for me. That will always be enough for me. If at some point when we are not both feeling emotional you want to sit down and discuss it, we can, but not right now."

Silent nodded, because there was still a hand covering his mouth, and Dox grinned at him. After being let go, Silent looked around, realising that they were already in the oak woods, but that they had veered off the path of torches that had been placed. Pointing that out to Dox, they started to look to the right and left, hoping to see the gleam of a torch in the distance. Seeing nothing, they agreed to keep walking straight, and hoped they would find something familiar soon. Picking up the pace slightly, trying to make sure they would have as much time as possible in the light if they had to backtrack, they both kept their eyes peeled.

A little while later, Dox spotted a light towards the right. Trusting their slightly stronger eyesight, Silent changed direction, pinging in the direction that they had pointed. The sudden appearance of lava in his path caused him to stumble to a halt, arm flinging out to stop Dox.

"Light yes, torch no."

"Okay, so I might have been wrong, but look across there!"

Looking over the patch of lava, Silent could see that there was a dark shape in the middle made of a dark material, a broken rectangular shape. It looked as though a section of it had been broken off. Looking back to the lava in front of them, Silent moved round to the left slightly, able to see a route that he could probably take through it. Jumping over the first patch, he looked for the next exposed area to jump. Continuing on the slightly zig zagged path through the lava, he quickly made it across, Dox following slightly behind.

Seeing a chest next to the structure, Silent moved towards it, while Dox studied the stone that it was made out of, noticing the golden blocks dug into the ground beside it and sat above it. Opening the chest, Silent found a golden sword, golden armour that seemed to be for a horse, and a golden apple. Taking all items and packing them away, he turned to meet Dox's excited eyes.

"Do you think this is one of them?" they asked.

"One of what?" Confusion was clear in his voice.

"A broken portal. If it is, I can so clearly see how it goes together and how to either build one or repair this, and then light it to see how it works!" The gears in Dox's head were so clearly working on everything they could discover from this and how it worked, that Silent could do nothing but nod, his slight apprehension forcefully pushed to the back of his mind.

"We can leave a torch path as we head home, so that we can find our way back later."

Pulling the reluctant Dox away from the ruined portal, they carefully made their way back across the lava, and headed hopefully towards home. Knowing that they were at least heading south, which was the rough direction of home, they continued, placing torches as they went. They moved through the trees, which slowly started to thin out, although the sky was also starting to darken. Luckily, in the fast-approaching twilight, they could see a light to the left, and moving towards it, they could see that it was the torch path that would lead them home. Pausing briefly to place an additional torch so that they could see where to veer off to the portal, the duo headed towards home. They reached the edge of the tree line as true night fell, and seeing the glow of the torches surrounding their home, they put on a final burst of speed. Pulling open the wonky gate, Silent gestured for Dox to go ahead of him, and following, he secured the gate. Making it to the front door which Dox had left open for him, he found them standing by the bar, deep in thought.

Pulling out a potato to eat, he enjoyed the *cronch* sound it made as he devoured it before moving onto a second one. Watching Dox, he could practically see the thoughts flickering across their face as they tried to process everything that had happened over the past few days. Humming a wordless tune, Silent started to remove his armour, noticing an arrow in the back of the chest plate.

"Huh… didn't even feel that."

Storing it in his personal storage, he considered, not for the first time, the combination of skill, magic, and science that had created what was basically a personal mini pocket dimension. The talent that Dox had for creating things really was a gift, and he was glad that they were there waiting for him on the day they left. It would be a colder life without them.

The subtle shifting of position made him notice that his Paradox was back in the present, and now watching him as he looked through them into the past. Glancing away awkwardly, he put away the rest of the potatoes that he had just been holding.

"So, what's our plan?"

Moving over to the chests and the crafting table, they pulled out the diamonds that they had, and some of the gold. Settling in to craft the diamonds into a pair of helmets, and the gold into two pairs of boots, Dox explained their idea.

"I really want to look into the enchanting of books that can be done, and the fact that we can apparently make a table that can be used with that blue stone you found… lapis, I think… to enchant things like armour and weapons and to store them into books. You can use an anvil apparently to combine them, but only a few times otherwise you weaken them. The amount of iron that will be needed for that is high, so that can be a secondary plan. I am also really interested in fixing and going through the portal. We have a diamond pickaxe, and there is some of the black stone at the bottom of the mineshaft. Looking at the portal we found, I think we would only need about four pieces. I can make a flint and steel for us to light it. I managed to buy you an enchanted diamond chest plate and leggings that are unbreakable and fire resistant, so that should be really helpful. I am making two diamond helmets so that we both have that extra protection. The guy also said that the natives that live there will ignore you if you are wearing gold, so I am making gold boots for us both. I intend to take a bow and do some distance fighting, while we both know that you like to get close and stab things, so you get the stronger armour."

"Okay, that makes sense. Do you know how to make the table to enchant things and the anvil? Would it be better for us to mine as much as we can? And maybe you can use the voodoo stuff to make your armour stronger too?"

Pausing from where they had just finished making the boots, they thought about it, looking at the ten diamonds that they had.

"If I made us gold helmets and diamond boots, I should have enough with two diamonds? I will need three pieces of the black stone, and I need to make a book, but we planted the sugarcane that I could use. For stronger enchantments I will need some bookcases, but if I see how many books I can make, between the thirteen bits of leather you have magically accumulated over the last few days, it might be enough."

"So, tomorrow when we get up, I will head to the bottom of the mines to dig up the stone we need, and you can get mining? Do we have enough iron left over?"

"I think so, and iron should be a quick fix if we don't. I am going to go and grab some of the sugar cane. Hopefully pruning it down will encourage more to grow."

Separating, Silent headed up the stairs towards his room, while Dox headed out to the pond. At the pond, the sugarcane had grown massively. Mentally thanking the laws of the land that caused the speedy growing, they chopped off the top third of the plant, and then the second third, leaving the bottom to grow. They had planted nine of the plants and had eighteen chunks of sugarcane. Walking back into the house, they stored in by the crafting table, and pulling out a potato to eat, walked upstairs. They had a lot of plans for the next few days and wanted to be well rested for them, so they would head to bed now and get an early start to the morning.

Closing the door to their room, they listened, hearing nothing but the creak of Silent's bed through the wall as he shifted to a comfortable position. Once again thinking about needing windows and contemplating the sand by the pond that could be used, they drifted off to sleep.

Chapter 11

Getting up the next morning, Silent stretched and wandered from their room and to the stairs. He could hear Dox moving around in their room, and leaving them to it, he started down the stairs, crossing the room to the kitchen. Rooting through the chests, he decided that he would take a stack of potatoes with him, the diamond pickaxe, and diamond sword. Moving away from the chest, he pulled on his armour, shouting out to Dox as he crossed to the front door. Pushing the door open, he let it swing closed immediately, walking back to the kitchen and grabbing a shield. Dox would be unhappy if they had to pull more arrows out of him or his iron armour. Heading back to the door, they passed Dox as they headed to the kitchen. Smiling at each other, neither were one for talking too early in the morning.

Heading down into the mine was becoming a common route now, and the stairs down were easy enough, breaking the blockage that was left at the bottom from last time. Moving through the lit passages, he was happy to note that there did not seem to be any creatures down there with him, although he could hear the angry hiss of the spiders through the wall that they had put up to block them. Making it to the steps down to the bottom without incident, he headed to where the water was flowing, bracing against the current, and started to hack into the black stone. A few minutes later, and he was starting to give up hope when the chunk cracked and broke off, allowing him to pick it up and look at it.

"No wonder it is so hard to mine... this is obsidian, or something very like it."

Hoping that he would be able to mine enough without breaking the pickaxe, he continued, losing track of time while the repetitive motion of the pickaxe lulled him into a trance. Unsure how much time had passed, he checked how much he had mined, and seeing thirteen pieces of obsidian, decided that it should be plenty, and headed back to the stairs. Halfway up, he heard a tell-tale sizzle, and looking behind him, he could see one of the green explosive creatures following him up the stairs. Not wanting them to damage the stairs, he sped up, running far enough from the stairs before he stopped. Turning, the creature was much closer than he thought, already puffed up to explode. Bracing himself behind his shield, he weathered the explosion as it came, still being knocked back a few paces, and a little battered. Pulling out a potato to assist with his healing he turned back towards the exit. Focused on the sound of his munching, he didn't hear anything behind him until he was hit from behind, feeling poison flooding his system. Spinning, he could see that where the creature had exploded, he had opened the wall that they had sealed, allowing two of the spiders to escape. Making a snap decision to close the gap and stop any more before fighting, he grabbed a few of the loose blocks that were in the centre of the explosion and started to build the wall back. The attack of the second spider was just as vicious and pushed more poison into him. Managing to place the last section of wall, he swapped to his sword, just as the first attacked him again. Swinging his sword to attack, he was startled by the fatigue that had set in. Luckily, the first spider only needed one hit to end it. Managing to block the next attack from the remaining spider, Silent got another good hit in, before the poison caused him to stumble, allowing the spider to get passed his guard again. A final swing of his sword managed to kill the spider, but it had also taken the last of his strength. Sword clattering to the floor, Silent dropped to his knees, the poison sapping his strength and health. Feeling everything slowly slip from his grasp, the magic of the pocket dimension was unable to hold anything with no strength in him left to maintain it. With no thought but to get to Dox, Silent started the long crawl back to home, vision dark around the edges, and limbs shacking as he crawled.

Passing Silent as he left the house had been surprising, because Dox was sure he had shouted goodbye a few minutes earlier, but knowing that they were somewhat forgetful, they brushed it off. Moving into the kitchen, and over to the chest where they had stored the eighteen bits of sugarcane in the night before, they pulled them out and took them to the crafting table. Laying them out, they realised that the easiest way to use them would be to combine three pieces horizontally. That way, the three together would create the right length of paper, and the width could be cut into three, getting three evenly sized bits of paper out of it. Getting started, they combined and split all of the cane until they were left with eighteen pieces of paper. Moving to grab the leather, they established that by folding and combining the paper with the leather, they could have a reasonably sized book from three pieces of the paper they had made, and a piece of the leather to combine them. Happy to have been able to make six books fairly quickly, they headed out to the pond again, delighted that overnight the sugarcane seemed to have regrown, allowing them to harvest eighteen more pieces. About to walk away, they thought about the bookshelves they wanted to make for the enchanting table, knowing that they would need three books each, and with three more bits of sugarcane they could make the additional book that they would need for the enchanting table. Pulling up the bottom third of three of the plants, Dox headed back to the house, setting a mental reminder to plant more next time they were able to harvest it.

Once they were back at the crafting table, they quickly started to make the paper for the books before moving on to combine it with the leather. Setting the books to one side, Dox took some of the remaining wood, stripping it down to make planks. Once they had plenty of planks, they took the books back to the crafting table, and started to make them into bookshelves with the planks. Moving through their tasks surprisingly quickly, they were soon taking the books up to the room that they had previously set to one side to make a workshop room. They placed the four bookshelves into the start of a half-moon shape, with the intention of placing the enchanting table in the centre.

Once they had placed everything, they headed back down to the crafting table to make an anvil, pulling the left-over iron out of the chest that they had placed it in after returning from the village. They had taken thirty-six ingots home with them, and using twenty-seven, they would be able to make the three blocks of iron they would need, and another four ingots to combine, and they should be fine, leaving five ingots spare. Creating the blocks first, they then added the last of the ingots before taking the completed anvil upstairs to rest near the enchanting table and library.

Knowing that there was nothing really left to do until they had the black stone, they moved outside to start doing a little bit of farming. Heading to the farm area, they pulled the first potato plant. As they went to replant one of them, they heard a sound from over by the mine. Instantly on guard and on the lookout for monsters, they span, switching to their bow as they did, an arrow at the ready.

They nearly loosed the arrow out of shock as crawling from the mine was not a monster, but Silent. As he slowly made his way from the edge of the mine towards the house, Dox ran to help him. They had only seen him in this state twice; once on the first day they met, and once after a job gone wrong. His last assassination.

Helping him stagger to his feet, they half carried him into the tavern. Their plans to pull out one of the spare travel plans were dashed when he single-mindedly turned towards the stairs. Being that he could not really stand without assistance, it was an impressive feat. Making sure they had a good grip on him, they started to make their way up the stairs. Several long minutes later, they hit the landing, and stumbling across to his room he was quick to tumble into bed. Dox knew that as scary as this was, he would be fine with a little rest and some food. Giving him some of their potatoes was a simple enough fix, which they did before they left the room and headed back downstairs.

Hitting the ground floor, they realised that when this had happened in the past, he was unable to hold onto any of his things and had left them where he was attacked. Thinking logically, he was going to be out for a little while. That would give Dox enough time to head down to the mine and collect his things. If they were careful, they could sneak in, grab them, and leave, avoiding the danger if Silent hadn't already killed it. Speeding outside and down into the mine, they reached the gap leading into the mine and took the path towards the ravine. Keeping a careful eye on their surroundings, they checked before going around every corner, ears pricked for any danger or sound. Hearing the scuttle of a spider, they span towards the wall that they had built to block out the spiders. As they did, they stumbled into a small hole that looked like something had exploded in it. On the edge of the whole was a spread pile of Silent's things. Moving towards the pile, they could see that the point of the explosion seemed to be right next to the spider wall. They assumed that the wall must have been damaged and that Silent had repaired it, probably while ignoring the fact that he was being attacked by something. Shacking their head with a small smile, they began to collect everything that he had dropped, taking extra care to make sure they had the diamond sword and pickaxe and the black stone. They would hate for him to be injured for nothing. After gathering everything, they turned to head back, pulling out a piece of the black stone to look at it as they started the trip back. Being able to hold it, they could see that it was actually obsidian, and they marvelled at the amount of effort that Silent must have put into mining it. That probably had something to do with him getting into the state he did. Knowing him, he didn't think to eat anything, was heading home already fatigued and was then snuck up on by an explosive monster before having spiders escape and attack him. Ignoring them to fix the wall he must have left himself able to kill them before collapsing.

Absolutely convinced that Silent would give them the same version of events when they got home, they realised that they were at the bottom of the stairs. Heading up the first two, they turned around to block off the entrance before bounding up the rest of them, across to the front door before going up to check on Silent. As they had expected, he was already pushing himself up and out of bed. He might be reckless, but at least he healed fast.

Walking up to him, they unceremoniously dumped nearly everything that they had picked up for him at his feet.

"What happened?"

"I was attacked by a creeper and a couple of spiders and they did more damage than I expected."

The fairly formal way that he had phrased that, along with the fact that he wouldn't quite make eye contact told them that there was slightly more to that story.

"What I am hearing is that you were heading home already fatigued because you forgot that eating is a thing your body needs, then met one of the explosive monsters, which released the spiders, which attacked, and you ignored them to fix the wall, and once that was fixed, you killed them before collapsing? Fairly close?"

"You didn't have to say it like that!"

"But am I wrong?"

"...No."

Grinning in victory, Dox swept out of the room, choosing to ignore Silent's muttering about overconfident platonic partners. They headed back downstairs, having kept the obsidian and the thirty books (that he had clearly stolen from the village) which would make an additional ten bookshelves after a quick trip out to the woods again to collect the extra wood that they would need. After running out to the woods with the axe, they noticed that it would be dark soon; so, quickly focusing on chopping down the trees for the wood that they would need, they headed back at a run, making sure that the wonky gate was securely closed. Having already made some bookshelves, making the next ten was easy enough. They ran the bookshelves upstairs, completing one level of the half moon and adding the second and some of a third while thinking about how to make the enchanting table work the best.

They decided that a base of the obsidian, combined with the diamonds would make the table, with the book able to rest on the top, infused with whatever magic this land had. Reaching the crafting table, they pulled out the materials, and after placing them carefully, they started to combine them. As they finished by placing the book on top, they flinched away as the book rose into the air slightly, hovering over the table. Excited, they grabbed the diamond sword and some lapis and carried everything up into the room, placing the book into the centre of the bookshelves. Placing the sword on the table, and the lapis into a small slot on the table, they looked inside the book. There were three options in there; the first one said bane of Arthropods, the second one said Knockback and the third said Unbreaking. As they went to see if there was anything on another page, they heard a noise at the door. Jolting slightly, they brushed their hand over the word 'unbreaking'. As they did, one of the pieces of lapis glowed and was absorbed into the sword, giving the sword a slightly eerie glow, and they felt a slight drop to their energy levels. Turning to face Silent, who had entered behind them, they saw him staring wide-eyed at the sword. His eyes flickered up to Dox, back to the sword, and back again.

"I want!"

"You want?"

"I want."

Laughing, Dox held out the sword to him, but he moved past them while pulling his own diamond sword and placing it on the table. Frowning, he looked at the book.

"How does it work?"

"You just press the option you want."

"What options? It is blank?"

Moving to look at the book, Dox could see that it was indeed blank. Taking the sword from him and placing it themselves, they could see that there were now only the first two options. Going over the interaction that they had with the Librarian, they had a thought.

"They mentioned that it takes energy to enchant things, and that you gain this energy from the mining of certain things, and by killing things here, you take some of their energy. What if when you were attacked and injured that badly, you lost that energy? And I felt a slight shift in mine just then. Maybe you have to get that energy to a certain level for it to work?"

"Kind of like that place we went to, where they span the wheel thing enough and it created static energy that they could harness to power things? Some things needed more energy than others, but if you disconnected the wires, you'd have to start again?"

"Yes, which they only discovered because you wanted to know what a wire did, and pulled it out."

"But Dox Darling. I was curious."

Not really having an answer to that, and knowing that 'curiosity killed the cat' would only lead to him saying that 'satisfaction brought it back', they moved on, ignoring his smirk. Walking back past Silent, they headed out of the room and back downstairs.

After waking up in his bed, Silent realized that he must have blacked out slightly somewhere after he had killed the spider. It would not be the first time it had happened, his survival instincts conserving power by shutting down everything but the need to get somewhere safe. Having Dox come in and practically throw his things at him showed him how worried they had been about him. The brief conversation that they had just proved that fact. Hearing them moving about downstairs before he heard the door open and close spoke volumes to him, knowing that they probably needed to get out of the house for a little bit. Slowly gathering all of his things from where they had landed, he started to put them away, noticing that the obsidian and the books were missing. Hoping that Dox had them, he started to sort everything into some sort of order within his pocket dimension. His armour was fairly damaged, but his sword still seemed to be okay. He made sure that his torches and food were easily accessible, and that his armour, even damaged, could be pulled on quickly. His diamond pickaxe was placed in a chest by his bed. Hearing movement through the door, he looked to see if Dox was on their way in. When the footsteps didn't pause at his door, Silent's curiosity took hold. Leaving his room, he headed towards the movement.

Pushing the door open slightly, he could see Dox bent over a floating book, jumping forwards slightly and knocking the book as they turned towards the door. As he watched, an apology on his lips for startling them, something blue on the table glowed and merged with the sword, which he hadn't noticed before. The sword started to give of a slight glow. Staring at the sword, he could feel Dox looking at him and he tore his eyes away from the sword to look at them, before looking back to check it was still glowing, then back to Dox.

"I want!"

"You want?"

"I want."

Dox laughed an offered the sword, but he stepped past them while grabbing his diamond sword and placing it on the table. Staring at the blank book, he called to Dox.

"How does it work?"

"You just press the option you want."

"What options? It is blank?"

Dox took over and tried to place the sword themselves,

which allowed two options to appear.

After briefly discussing the potentials of energy usage being the issue here, Dox left to head back downstairs, a response on their lips, silenced probably by the knowledge that Silent could never help but have a response to everything.

Chapter 12

After following Dox out of the room and downstairs, Silent took a seat at the table closest to the kitchen.

"Dox, if we plan to make a trip to the other place tomorrow, we should probably decide what we are going to take with us."

Mild agreement noises filtered out to him through the kitchen, and he could hear them moving around within there. After a few moments of waiting, he decided to head in, to speak to them and plan. Opening the door, he walked into... a boat.

"Ummm..."

"I want us to be prepared for every eventuality. And that includes a boat. I don't want to swim for ages."

"Okay, what else do you want us to have?"

"Plenty of food; we don't know how long we will be there. Two axes and pickaxes each, in case we have to clear a path. At least one full slot on the pocket dimension of stone; we might need to build a staircase, and that should be just over sixty each. The same number of torches too; if it gets dark, I want to keep the monsters away and be able to see. Two of us will fit in a boat so we should only need one between us, and I'll carry it. Some obsidian, just in case. I made a flint and steel earlier, so that should come too. Obviously, the diamond and golden armour, and maybe a makeshift crafting table and some spare gold. Oh, and some travel beds! I think that is it?"

"Okay, that is a lot! And I am guessing that you want to take as much from there as you can?"

"Yes. Oooh, and I need a bucket."

They hurried back to the crafting table, storing the boat, and pulling out some of the last bits of iron.

"We only have enough for the bucket, not for the axes or pickaxes," said Dox.

"Didn't you make a few and store them?"

"I did?"

Walking over to the chests, they pulled them out in victory.

"I did. I am so organised!"

Under his breath, Silent muttered

"Yeah, so organised you forgot about it."

"Sorry, hunny, what was that?" The dangerous edge to their voice had him backtracking.

"Oh, nothing at all, just commenting that I doubt we have forgotten anything that we need to bring."

"Hmm… sure you were."

Walking back over to Silent, they started to quickly pass them the pickaxes… followed by everything else.

Silent started gathering everything up, trying to keep everything in some type of order with the food and weapons in easy reach, and armour set to be put on as soon as they were out of the tavern.

"Do you want me to carry the bucket, gold, and crafting table, as you have the boat?"

"No, I have the boat and everything else I might need because you get distracted or bored and wander off."

"Okay that's fair, but you didn't have to say it!"

"Yes, yes, I think I did. Okay, I have everything from my side, I think. Is there anything else you want or need?"

"No, I think I'm good. You want to head out now?"

Without answering, Dox headed through the kitchen door

and towards the front door. Stepping outside, he started to pull on his armour, seeing Dox start to head to the gate.

"Dox Darling, armour."

Hearing what might have been a muffled curse, he watched as they turned away from the gate, and ran back towards the door, disappearing inside. Laughing, Silent finished putting his armour on, admiring the diamond, and enjoying the feeling of extra protection. A minute later, Dox reappeared and started to pull on their armour. Opening his mouth to start to say something, Dox's eyes snapped to him.

"Not a word."

He closed his mouth.

Both armoured up, they headed to the gate together, giving it an extra shove to make it move. After stepping through and then making sure it was fully secured behind them, they headed towards the tree line. Following the torch path from this route was much easier, and they quickly reached the fork in the torch path, heading right to follow the path to the broken portal.

The final stretch before they hit the lava went surprisingly quickly, and they were some jumps between patches of lava. After making it to the clear stretch in the centre, Dox pulled out the obsidian. Studying the remains of the pillar, Dox could see where it had shattered, and how to slot the new pieces into it. Starting with the lowest one, which they could reach, they slotted it in, making sure that it was a seamless join. Using the cobblestone they had, they made a rough staircase allowing them to reach the top section that needed fixing. Placing in the other two needed blocks, and again making sure that the join was smooth, they climbed back down. Pulling out a pickaxe, they took down the staircase before replacing everything.

Giving the portal one final check, they grabbed the flint and steal, and struck, aiming for the middle block on the inside of the portal. The portal **whooshed** as it came to life, causing them both to jump backwards. A purple haze filled the previously empty hole in the portal, swirling around.

"I'll go first," said Silent. "If you don't hear me screaming, head in after?"

Nodding at Silent, Dox watched as he stepped into the swirling portal. The noise of it intensified as Silent slowly faded from view.

The portal noise increased around him as he took that first step into the portal, knowing that he would never send Dox first if he could avoid it, especially if there might be danger ahead. The world went dark before the sound started to change. He heard the portal, but also the crackle of flames and the hiss of lava, and underneath all that, a soft grunt... a familiar grunt. Breath starting to grow ragged, Silent pulled out his sword just as the portal cleared, and he stepped out. Spread out ahead of him was an expanse of red. Lava seemed to sprout from everywhere, and scattered around him, were them.

Heart starting to pound, the sound of the lava was drowned out by the blood that seemed to be roaring through his body, blocking his ears and tinging his vision red. There they stood, calmly watching him, their pig-like faces mocking him, some in armour, some without, some with weapons and some without. A cold fear spread through his system. These creatures were evil. He knew what they did to an innocent creature. What would they do to his Paradox?

With fear fuelling his rage, Silent turned to the closest creature, cutting it down with his sword. As his weapon made contact, a rage blindness spread over him. The others in the area moved towards him with aggression. He allowed his body to take over — he had been training for this for years. Cutting a path through the creatures as they stepped up to him, he revelled in the feeling of power, and the knowledge that he was no longer powerless. Like a berserker, there was no awareness of injury to him. Adrenaline kept him moving faster than they could stop him, the battle getting easier as their numbers thinned out. He could vaguely hear something that could have been someone calling out, but he was deaf to the world. As he finished with the last one in the area, he stumbled to a halt, eyes darting around for more, starting to move away to track them down, when he froze in shock. From behind him was a shout, full of concern and some fear.

"SI!"

Turning, he locked eyes with Dox before his eyes dropped down to their hand, eyes widening past their usual point.

After Silent had stepped through the portal, Dox had watched as the spiralling slowed and the noise returned to a standard level. Giving Silent a couple of minutes, they stepped up to the edge of it before taking the final step into it. As the portal noise rose up around them, they watched for the change of terrain, and after the darkness of the portal cleared, it was obvious that they were in a very different place.

Hearing a commotion to the left, they spun slightly, and saw a mass of the pig like creatures — Piglin, the villagers called them — crowded around something fighting. A slice of a sword clearing a gap allowed them to see Silent. His face twisted into something violent as if a bloodlust had overtaken him. His body was tight with rage, and every line of his body seemed to seep violence. Remembering his attempt at telling them his tale, they wondered if they should have let him. Clearly it was much worse than they had believed if this was what happened, and it was clearly done by this species.

A soft grunt sounded from next to them. Looking to the right, they saw nothing, before another soft grunt and a shuffle made them look down, and let out a gasp. There, watching the massacre of what was probably their family and community, was a young child.

Stepping closer to the child, their heart broke as he flinched away from them. Holding their palms up and empty, they slowly shuffled closer, until they were able to put their hands on his shoulders, offering a paltry comfort when considering what he was watching. Turning the child to face them and away from the slaughter, they held him there before calling out to Silent, trying to get him to stop. Nothing that they shouted seemed to have any affect however, and if it wasn't for the fact that the villagers had said that any Piglin that pass through the portal would turn to zombies, Dox would have left with him then and there.

Keeping an eye on the fight, they could see that there were no longer any Piglin standing. However, Silent was glancing around, eyes hunting for his next target. As he went to start off in one direction, Dox shouted again.

"DON'T YOU DARE! YOU BETTER BE HEARING ME NOW, SILENT! SI!?"

At the last word, an old nickname of his that he had asked them to never use, he startled and turned, staring at them, before his eyes dropped to the child. He took a step forward, sword still in his hand, eyes still vaguely empty.

"No. Stop. Si. This is a child. One whose entire family is now gone. We are going to be looking after him. Us coming here is the reason he is alone, and therefore he is our responsibility."

"Congrats, I'm a dad?"

His voice was cracked and broken, a slight tremor running

through it, but it was his voice. Letting out a sigh of relief, Dox shifted so that they were no longer blocking most of the child from view. Looking down at him, Dox asked.

"What is your name?"

"Dox, I am fairly positive that they don't speak our language," said Silent.

"We will call you Oliver, then. It means peace or kind one. And you will be the start of peace between Silent and this place."

Glaring at Silent as though daring him to disagree, he held his hands up, made slightly worse by the sword held in it. That caused Oliver to flinch away, hiding behind Dox, and they could see the moment that the guilt, pain, and heartbreak finally hit Silent, when he saw that his rage had led to this moment, where an innocent child was flinching from him making a simple movement.

In an effort to give himself some distance, he put away his sword and pulled out the cobblestone.

"I will make us a quick protective shelter to make sure that we can keep him safe." His voice sounded dull and defeated, none of his usual energetic tone. Starting to put a wall into place, he swiftly placed the first layer around them before hopping up onto the first to start to place the second. After doing the same to make the third layer, he jumped down, bracing himself for the impact. Turning to Dox, keeping his eyes firmly above shoulder level, he asked,

"Do you have any wood on you?"

"Ummm, yes, one sec, let me grab it."

Trying to dig it out of their pocket dimension, they accidentally threw the boat on the floor. Ignoring it for the moment, they passed the wood over to him along with a crafting table before turning to the boat. Startling, they saw that Oliver had sat down in the boat, and was calmly watching them.

After placing the crafting table, he used the wood to piece together a door. After making the door, he picked it up, pulling out his pickaxe as he did, and quickly stripped out one section of the bottom two layers of the wall, collecting the cobblestone, and fitting the door in place. After making sure that it opened and closed properly, he moved on to start putting a secure roof on. It was not the largest roof, but it would at least protect the young child that he had orphaned. In the background as he slotted cobblestone in place to start to form the roof, he could hear Dox talking to him, trying to convince him to do something. Resolutely ignoring the situation, determined to do what was necessary after causing the situation, but nothing more, he continued building.

"Oliver, please get out of the boat…"

Nothing, just those innocent eyes staring at them blankly.

"Please, I know you don't understand me, but I need you to not just stay in the boat."

Trying to mime getting out of the boat, they continued. They offered him a potato to see if he would follow for food. Nothing.

Placing their head in their hand, they considered the next options.

"If we are leaving you in here, I guess you can keep the boat if you like it so much?"

Sighing, they stood up, noticing that it was getting darker. Looking around, they could see that Silent was well on his way to finishing the roof for the little shelter. Pulling out some torches, Dox started to light up the area, making sure that Oliver wouldn't end up in darkness. As they placed the last one, they turned to see Silent standing awkwardly in the corner of the shelter, looking at the door like it was his lifeline, or more accurately, his escape route. Stepping into both his line of sight and escape path, he focused on Dox. Voice stiff and formal, and devoid of emotion, he spoke again.

"This is not going to be a good permanent location for us to use for him, Dox. He will need more than a boat. We should find someone to take him in."

"Silent... I know this is a lot right now, and there is clearly a lot that I don't know about the situation, but look at him. Really look at him, and tell me that you could leave him with a stranger?"

Staring at Dox for a long moment, he sighed, turned away, and walked closer to the... to Oliver. Crouching down so that he was on his level, he looked at his features, and heard the grating grunting that haunted his dreams, holding himself still to avoid pulling away, or doing something more regretful. Finally, his eyes dropped to meet Oliver's eyes. In them was a childlike wonder, an innocence that time and the people you meet strip away from you. And also, deeper, barely understood, was a deep and encompassing sadness, so similar to the one that he had seen in the mirror before he found Dox. Something gave inside him, the untying of a knot, or the crumbling of a wall. His eyes, still locked with the pure innocence in front of him, filled with tears, slowly seeping out and down his cheek. A new feeling started to fill his heart, spreading determination throughout his entire being. Instinctively, he tried to squash this new and strange protective urge, but he stopped himself, realizing that for the first time, this was a feeling untainted and pure, no altruistic emotions linked to it.

"Hello, Oli. I'm going to be your dad, now. I will protect you always. Nothing will harm you, and you will never again need to feel the pain that I have caused you today."

The solemnness of the promise and the raw emotion in their platonic spouse's voice brought tears to Dox's eyes. Taking a steadying breath, they walked over to him where he was kneeling and placed a hand on his shoulder.

"We both will."

And there, staring down at the young child whose life they had turned upside down, a family was born.

Printed in Great Britain
by Amazon

83755293R00068